SIDEWAYS AND BACKWARDS

A Novel of Time Travel and Self Discovery

Heather Teysko

ISBN-13: 978-0986354526

This book is dedicated to my fellow music history geeks
in the world. I'm always on the lookout for you.

And my dear husband and daughter.
I love you both so much.

ACKNOWLEDGEMENTS

Many thanks goes to National Novel Writing Month; without the discipline and creative freedom they provide, this novel would never have happened. And to all the NaNoWriMo participants who cheer each other on via twitter and the message boards each year. Thank you!

Thank you to the listeners of my podcast, the Renaissance English History Podcast, for your constant support and listenership. I value you more than you can imagine.

Thank you to the beta readers and everyone who provided thoughtful feedback and criticism via Wattpad on the rough draft of the book. Many of you are also mamas who took valuable reading hours to give me thoughtful feedback on my book. Thank you so much.

Thank you to Tribe Writers and Jeff Goins for giving me the courage to publish, and a community of supportive writers who lift each other up, and provide a constant cheering section for any new creative endeavor.

Thank you to Joy Hoppenot, a brilliant developmental editor, for her feedback and help through a scary process.

Thank you to Morten Lauridsen, for writing music that can transport us to other worlds if we just listen in quiet stillness.

And finally, thank you to my family. My husband, Jonathan who loves me unconditionally, and gives me space and time to write. And the amazing Hannah Zen, who inspires me to live a life of creativity and adventure because I want her to see her mama setting an example for her.

Table of Contents

Sideways and Backwards

A Novel of Time Travel and Self Discovery

CHAPTER ONE

In Which Things Fall Apart

Normally I really like these autumnal misty mornings where the fog lays heavy on the ground in the same way my duvet is weighing me down, making any persuasion to get out of bed seem dull and unimportant. Today, though, there is a huge clash going on. An epic battle between the dreamworld in which I was living not five minutes ago, filled with warmth and quiet; and the incessant beeping of my phone. Someone clearly wants to tell me something, and I can't decide whether it's worth it to make the effort required to reach it, charging on my night table, which requires movement.

Last night was Halloween - a night filled with debauchery and revelry, when the spirits all come out to play, uninhibited by normal societal mores. It would take several dozen pints of alcohol to equal the inhibition-destroying capabilities of one single Halloween party where everyone is hidden behind costumes and masks, and feeling both frisky, and free to act on their friskiness.

Honestly, I'm not sure that I even want to read whatever texts or Facebook tags or Instagrams or Snapchats people are sending me. The first half of the night is clear; a loft party in Tower Bridge. The second half gets a little hazy, and I honestly think it would be better not clarified in my head. Not for the first time in recent history, I smack my face, and groan that I will never touch alcohol again.

At least I'm alone in my own bed, which means that I didn't bring anyone home. I sigh into my pillow and pull the duvet back up over my head. I can't face it. There isn't enough Nurofen in every Boots in London to make my headache go away. The rain patters on the window. All I want in the world right now is a nice cup of coffee. And ibuprofen. And maybe a greasy breakfast. Why do I keep doing this, I wonder. Aren't I getting a little bit old for this kind of partying? Is this really how I want to be acting at age 35 (though in fairness to me, I tell everyone I meet I'm 28)?

This isn't the first time that I've gone off the deep end. In fact, episodes like last night are becoming disturbingly more frequent, something I can admit when I'm feeling like this the morning after. I am regressing. I'm 35 with a demanding job in as an Editor-in-Chief of a publishing house, and I have staff that depend on me and need me to be on my game, but every year I get closer and closer to acting like a crazy college student.

It wasn't always like this. I showed up in London from Los Angeles with wide eyes, basking in the literary capital of the world, feeling so excited about life. I went to museums and concerts at lunchtime. I took in life and culture. Breathed it in deeply. But then somewhere in my late 20s, it all seemed to go off course. Work got demanding. And there was the broken heart and then The Horrible Year, which I'm still not over yet. I'm clearly in avoidance.

The phone buzzes again, and is becoming persistent. Again and again it beeps and buzzes and rings. Someone clearly needs to talk to me. I muster all the energy I can, and throw my right arm down on the floor, bracing myself to lean over and get my phone. My Halloween costume is thrown across the sofa; I dressed as Britney Spears circa 1999 from her One More Time video. I thought it was so clever. I had the high knee socks, and Catholic-girl skirt down perfectly.

I do a modified warrior yoga pose, moan, and manage to get my phone without having to leave the warmth of my duvet. Let's just see what all of this is about...

Holy crap, there are approximately 187 messages and missed calls and Facebook tags and Instagram messages and...how do people keep up with this? It's like a job. I click on the first message, and there on my screen, in HD retina Technicolor glory, is a graphic picture of myself doing...oh my God, what am I doing, and who took this picture?

For a moment I'm too stunned to even think properly. And then it starts to get clear. Oh no. It all comes back to me, wave after wave, each one making me sink a little further into bed and a little more fearful of ever going outside my flat again. The grimy strip club somewhere around Euston we went after the party in Tower Bridge. The lap dances I got as a joke. The gorgeous Spanish girl who asked me if I wanted to go to the back room and get friendly. Me putting money into her g-string while my crew of friends laughed, and kept the alcohol flowing freely.

And here is a picture of me on Facebook with my tongue on another girl's nipple, clearly spanking her ass while she is grinding her g-string into my knee.

And the line of cocaine on the side table with my credit card right next to it having just cut it up.

That is not my cocaine, I swear to God.

Oh, this is bad. My grandmother is going to see this.

Why the hell would somebody take that picture, and why the hell would they post it on Facebook and why the hell would they tag me? The drugs aren't even mine. I've never lost that much control of my life. But according to this picture, I'm on a serious bender. For the love of God, who are the idiots I was out with last night, anyway?

I quickly untag myself and report the photo. Then I deal with the messages. I scroll through my texts. Mostly it's people asking whether I got home ok, and if I need anything, or if they can do anything for me. My mother is asking if I'm in trouble. My father...I can't read that one, let's just let that one go for another time.

I'm praying no one professional saw this yet, and force myself to open my work emails. No such luck, my guardian angel was clearly sleeping through the night just like me, and missed this opportunity to come to my rescue. My boss Howard, the CEO at Court Magician, our publishing company (named with a cheeky reference to John Dee, Queen Elizabeth I's court astrologer - we publish literary works that inspire and ignite imagination, the way our hero, John Dee did), emailed me this morning and wants to have a meeting on Monday morning about "the way I'm presenting my public face to my staff".

The headache that was already debilitating is threatening to render me unconscious.

Holy crap. This is bad. This is really bad. The awfulness of the situation is starting to settle in and I'm contemplating a new life living in a cave in Iceland when my phone buzzes again. Some stupid gossip website has picked up the site, and tagged Court Magician. Things just went from really uncomfortable to liability. Do I need a lawyer now?

My phone rings yet again, and when I gather up enough courage to check who it is, I see it's my best friend Sophie. There aren't many people I can handle right now, but she's one I can. Not only is she my best friend, but she's also head of PR for Court. She technically works for me, but I'm head of editorial and she's in marketing, so our paths don't cross that often, and I can still be friends with her.

"Sophie, I'm dying."

"No, you're not. You're just in a really bad spot right now." She's always straight to the point, and full of common sense.

"What happened last night?"

"I don't know Tasha. I left at a reasonable time. Clearly you got into some trouble."

"Sophie, I might get fired."

Sophie has a husband and young children, so she rarely comes out to play with me. That doesn't usually stop her from enjoying the stories I can tell, and living vicariously through me in a world that doesn't involve diapers and temper tantrums, but I can tell that this has gone too far even for her.

"Tasha, I run publicity, remember? I have all weekend to figure out a way to spin this. I've already contacted It's Hot magazine to get them to remove the pictures."

"Thank you," is all I can say in meek response.

"Now look, I don't have a lot of time. Ben wants his porridge and Hannah wants her waffles. And John is nowhere to be found. He's probably in the office starting at your pictures."

"Sophie, I'm so..."

"I know, you're sorry. Listen, I know you are, and I love you for it, and you're clearly a troubled soul, and all of that. I'm going to fix this for you because it's what I do for a living, but do me a favor, ok? Get out of London this weekend. Go somewhere to get some fresh air. Don't go out tonight. Don't go anywhere. Unless it's in the country. Go outside and do some thinking. Be an introvert. Please, for the love of God, turn off your phone, get out of London, and let me do my thing. After I give the kids breakfast. Ben, do not eat Hannah's waffle! Your porridge is almost ready!"

I promise her meekly that I will seek some peace and quiet somewhere outside of the city, though with the rain and clouds, the prospect of a country getaway seems dismal. I pull myself out of bed and take Sophie's advice to turn my phone off. I look at my Britney costume, which seemed so clever 12 hours ago, and I want to throw up. I pick the pieces up and toss them in the trash.

I trudge to the kitchen and get some coffee ready, and then fry up some eggs with toast. My cat, Wrigley, is also begging for some food, and so I pour some dry nuggets into the dish for her. I have a greasy breakfast, coffee, and a fat and content cat. I should be happier, but the breakfast just sits there, a lump in my stomach. I fear I might be sick if I keep eating it. Wrigley gives me a look of sympathy, but then remembers that she is a cat, and I am merely a hungover and shamefaced human, and so she goes back to her snuggly chair.

I head back up to my bedroom, and quickly pack for my weekend away, grabbing a backpack that I last used on a camping trip in Cornwall over the summer. Oh, that trip, I think. It was a group of us out there together on a farm a few miles from Penzance. I don't remember much about the weekend, though. I remember that it was cold, even though it was summer, and the evening turned to debauchery as has been the trend of my evenings lately. I woke up half clothed in a field at 5am, freezing, surrounded by cows, with an empty bottle of Jack Daniels and about ten of my new best friends I'd never met before. You'd think I'd have learned my lesson then. What can I say, I'm a slow learner, with deep demons.

I rush to throw some clothes, a few toiletries and my iPad and Kindle into a bag and then I put on jeans, boots, and a sweater. I grab my umbrella, and rain jacket, leave Wrigley some food for the weekend to which she nods her tepid approval, and I go out to face the world. With my sunglasses on. There's only so much of the world I can face without protection.

Normally I take cabs everywhere around London, but given the email from my boss I decide that today might not be a bad day to start being a bit more frugal. And anyway, the prospect of sitting in the back of a black cab whizzing around the crowded streets makes my stomach turn. Finally, I don't know where I even want to go. I wouldn't know where to tell the cabbie to take me. I know black cab drivers are meant to have the secret Knowledge of everything related to London, but even they can't read a mind that doesn't know itself.

The fresh air will do me good, and the rain is turning into more of a drizzle, so I walk through the Highgate Wood to the Highgate tube station, breathing in the moist scent of London, which I really do adore. Eight years ago I used to do this for fun. Back when I was still in love with London, and with myself, and my heart hadn't been wasted yet. The rain is pattering under my umbrella, and I cuddle into my coat, feeling sheltered, despite the mud.

Even though it's November 1, some of the trees are still this verdant shade of green that you only get in rainy England; a green that assaults your eyes with its fertility. The other leaves are various shades of golden orange and red, and are gathered in wet, soppy puddles on the side of the paths, a caretaker evidently having been through with a rake already this morning, though there was little he could do about the puddles and rain. I deeply breathe in the air, the moistness burrowing down into my chest, and feel slightly invigorated. Enough so that I can face the tube, which is bound to be wet, slippery, and full of other wet, miserable people.

I catch the first train headed south, one to Morden via Bank. I'm still not entirely sure where I'm going. The thought occurs to me that maybe it would be a good weekend to go to the seaside and wallow in the gales and windy rain. Perhaps I'll go to Waterloo and look at the timetables. Maybe somewhere like Chichester. Somewhere that had been through Roman, Viking, and Norman invasions, and still had the air of a conquered people about them, with the shame of having been the entry point of the Black Death in England. A place like that would seem very suitable to me right now.

The train lurches through Archway, and Tufnell Park. It's not crowded, being 11am on a Saturday when so much of London is hung over after Halloween festivals, and the weather is awful. I'm not looking forward to another November in London. The constant wet and damp of the rain. The onset of darkness. There is no place as special as England in June, but you pay for it when you're in England in November.

On we go through Camden and Euston, and I study the ads above the seats for various things like cheap mobile plans, car insurance, travel insurance, Vitamin C infused soda, and books I probably will never read, despite the fact that I read for a living. Then at King's Cross I'm pulled off the train. Not literally, but it just hits me that I don't want to go to the southern coast, but I want to go north. I want to go somewhere like Edinburgh or York. I want more darkness. Almost like doing a penance. I have this fantasy of escaping into the darkness, and having it cover me like a warm blanket where I don't have to face anyone. So appealing.

I make my way through the underground labyrinth of tunnels and escalators, maneuvering around tourists with giant suitcases, and students with giant backpacks, and pop up out of my subterranean world on the side of the station, with its shiny new shops and restaurants. I see a Burger King, and praise God that I can have more grease, which I can hopefully keep down. The morning is looking brighter already.

But first, a train. I walk to the center of the concourse and look up at the boards with updated times and schedules. The train to York has just left. But there are trains to Cambridge every fifteen minutes. Cambridge. The home of the ancient university, and great choirs. Since I moved to the UK ten years ago I've wanted to spend an extended amount of time in Cambridge, but I got busy with work and being a slobbery drunk, and never really spent that much time there other than for the occasional meeting, or punting day trip when family would visit. I should go to Cambridge. It's settled. I buy a ticket at the automated machines, wait in the queue for grease at Burger King, buy a Guardian newspaper and magazines at a WH Smith (no internet or phone for me all weekend; just old fashioned paper) and make my way through the gates to platform 11.

I realize as I'm walking through the station that being without my phone is giving me a chance to really look at my surroundings, and experience them without the normal distractions when I am staring at that little four-inch screen. Carrying my WH Smith bag, my Burger King brunch, and my weekend shoulder bag, I feel like I'm a teenager on a first backpacking adventure. Normally I'm running for trains, worrying about missing meetings, on the phone ordering my staff around, rushing through stations never looking at them. But look at the bricks here, the archways, the Victorian architecture. Feel the brisk November breeze whipping through the station. The pigeons feasting on discarded sandwiches in the trash. What a funny experience it is for me to walk through the station with my senses fully turned on for the first time in so many years.

It reminds me of when I first moved to London and everything was new and fresh and exciting, and ancient and historic, and full of wonder. Before I got jaded and started calling it the Big Smoke, and noticing all the little annoyances of everyday life. The narrow sidewalks haven't changed since I was 27 and thought they were quaint. What's changed is that I now rush through the streets trying to get somewhere. King's Cross used to mean Harry Potter and magical trains, and now it's just another anonymous underground stop that gets me closer to the office.

When did I get blown so off course, I wonder, finding my train and walking to the far end in hopes that I can get two seats to myself; maybe even with a table so that I can spread out my paper and my greasy second breakfast. When did life become such a struggle? When did I become such an alcoholic? And what the hell have I done to my career, which at one point several years ago seemed so promising? How on earth can I ever recover from this?

Well, I know the answer to those questions. All of them, really. But I can't deal with it. Not yet. I'm still in self-protection mode. If I let it go, the guilt and pain will consume me. I can't really get present to life without dealing with what happened half a decade ago, and I'm not ready to do that yet. Hey, at least I'm honest about it.

I step on to the train, get my empty tabled booth, and start to spread out. Breakfast unpacked here. Soda there. Newspaper unfolded here. The windows are foggy and have streaks and drops of water from the journey into King's Cross. I'm still wearing my sunglasses, and that, mixed with the ibuprofen I took this morning is making life seem a little less dismal, at least physically. At least I feel hungry. The egg, bacon, cheese and croissant mixed with the hash brown and doused with Diet Coke will also help enormously.

The automated woman's robot voice comes on, stilted and crisp. "Welcome aboard the 12:00 service to Cambridge. Calling at Finsbury Park, Stevenage, Hitchin, Letchworth, Baldock, Royston, and Cambridge. This train is ready to depart." Then the lights above the door flash, signaling their imminent closure. I look around the carriage, and there are only two other people besides myself, and they both look as dead to the world as I feel. At least my journey should be quiet. I take a bite out of my sandwich and watch as the train lurches forward, slowly picking up steam, and north London passes me by.

CHAPTER TWO

In Which I Arrive in Cambridge

As the train lurches forward slowly at first, I dig into my second breakfast, hearing my chewing in the silence of the train car. Off we go, past the suburbs of north London, where I have lived almost my entire time here. I see the Alexandra Palace up above Muswell Hill where I own my house now; it's a Victorian entertainment complex, and in all the time I've lived here, I've never seen anything there. Why is that? How can I have been so preoccupied, and with what, that I don't even see what's special in my own backyard? I make a mental note to check out their schedule this coming summer, and spend at least one evening on the lawn listening to music with strawberries and Pimm's.

Further on we go, past the outer suburbs. Barnet where I know there was a crucial battle in the Wars of the Roses, but that's pretty much all I know. I don't even know who won that battle. I must have known once, I suppose. I sigh and lean my head against the window, the cold glass refreshing on my overheated head. I used to inhale information like this. To be consumed by history and music and books. I'd care about the battle of Barnet. I'd read books about it.

Suddenly I'm feeling very claustrophobic in this train. It's like I'm having some kind of crazy panic attack or something. I'm shaking, and my heart is pounding in my chest like a sledgehammer. My head feels like it's going to explode. What am I going to do about work? What about my reputation? Do I need to leave London all together, start fresh somewhere else? And where would I go now? New York? Starting all over in my mid 30's in New York does not seem like an appealing option. I have to figure out a way to salvage this. I just have to.

I don't know what I can do, though. Sophie told me to keep my phone off, and that she would fix the bad publicity. And I trust her. The woman is amazing at her job. But how am I going to fix things with Howard, my boss, our publisher? What can I do to make this right? To show him that my days of acting like an entitled college kid with no inhibitions are over? That I'm turning over a new leaf? I need to grow up fast. I recognize it, and I need to own it, and think of a plan to make things right.

I start doing some deep yoga breathing I learned when I went through a new age phase, and was deep into chakras and tarot and pilates. I put my head down on the table on top of the newspaper, close my eyes, and take deep breaths, exhaling out in quick spurts the way the teacher taught us, and breathing in deeply. I give myself some loving self-talk. I have all weekend to hit on a solution, I think. It's noon on Saturday. I need to be in Howard's office at 9am on Monday. That means I have like 45 hours. I'm going to the country. I'm going to think and clear my head and breathe the clean air.

I have to trust that an answer will come to me. I have to believe it. I need to be on the lookout for answers. Watch and wait. When in doubt, watch and wait, and an answer will come. My breathing starts to return to normal. The conductor comes to check tickets, and I pull my head off the table, and manage a smile. I'm kicking myself for not buying a bottle of water, and only having this Diet Coke, but it will have to do. I sit up straight, I relax my back, and I order myself to pull it together.

I am a functioning adult, I tell myself. I am actually a highly functioning adult. I have a house on Woodland Gardens in Muswell Hill. I own it. Well, the bank owns it. But I was approved for the loan. It is decorated in a chic and elegant way thanks to the furniture shops on Tottenham Court Road. I am just going through a rough spot, I tell myself. But I will make it through this. I will turn my life around, and someday in a year or two or even five, I will look back at this period as a dark time, but I will have passed it. Breathe in the peaceful healing energy. Breathe out the negative energy. In with the good. Out with the bad.

I will start by reading the paper. I skip the news section and go straight to the arts and books parts, which interest me the most. There's an article about Elliot Smythson, an author I really wanted to land for Court Magician, but he went with Maplethorpe instead. They gave him a better deal, and while I tried my best to match it, in the end Howard didn't think he was worth the gamble since he was unknown at the time. Maplethorpe gave him a huge advance and promised 50,000 copies to be shipped along with major publicity and a book tour of 20 cities. Now the guy is everywhere from Oprah to the New Yorker to the Los Angeles Times Festival of Books.

And here he is on the front page of the Arts section of the Guardian giving an interview about how he became as successful as he is. For a long time I've ignored his success, finding it grating, and a reminder of my failure to secure him with Court. But maybe the new grown up adult me should read his interview, and perhaps I could even learn something from it. After all, this new me is trying to look for signs, and surely this is one?

I take a deep breath, and a bite of egg croissant, wipe the crumbs from my mouth, and start to read. It's largely the same pompous self-aggrandizement that I've come to expect from Elliot, who is smarter and brighter and better groomed than any other man in the entire world, according to him. Really, I'd love to learn a thing or two from his ego. But then there's an answer that stops even me.

The Guardian: "You've always been a dabbler in new age philosophies, right? Do you attribute your success to any of those beliefs or practices?"

This sort of makes me snort because Elliot never seemed particularly spiritual when we were negotiating contracts. More like he wanted more of a donation to be made to the Church of His Holy Authorship. But I read on, curious now.

Elliot Smythson: "Well, it's true that I've experimented with many new age and self help philosophies. I did the est training in the 80's, for example. I also have consulted with tarot card readers, past life healers, and other assorted mystics and psychics. The biggest thing I've learned through this is the importance of trusting your gut and following signs. There are signs everywhere that will lead you to your success if you just take the time to see them. Truly, they are everywhere. Synchronicity is the biggest untapped resource on the planet."

Well if that isn't the most self satisfying pile of bullshit I've ever heard. He got to be a bestseller giving Oprah advice because he followed signs? Not because he negotiated with balls of steel?

But then I remember that I am now trying to be mature, and looking for answers to my persistent problem of being an alcoholic (or at least having that reputation) and so I decide to think about it. What if I gave it a try? Followed signs and saw what happened? At least for the weekend. It couldn't hurt, right? It could be an interesting experiment that might give me something to think about; a context in which to come up with a solution to the problem of my impending pink slip at work.

I resolve to give it a try. I will spend the weekend following signs, and see what happens. As soon as we get to Cambridge.

I finish my fast food, and spend the rest of the train journey watching the rain come down in buckets over what were once the swampy fens. I'm going to have to find a cozy little bed and breakfast, and quick, I think, because I'm not going to last long if it's pouring like this all day. Eventually we roll through Baldock and Royston, and I see Cambridge come into view, the Cambridge University Press building on the left. I should read one of their books, I think. That could be a sign. I should read more intellectual books, and not just the pile of submissions that land on my desk. I should expand my horizons. Spend 20 minutes a day on something besides work reading. Go to museums. Learn things.

I remember the Cambridge University Press has a bookstore in the center of town; after I find my cozy bed and breakfast, I'll wander in and pick something out, and perhaps spend the afternoon tucked away in a coffee shop somewhere reading and being cozy. Just the thought of it warms me; it would be like the old days when I first moved to London and would spend hours in the Borders on Charing Cross Road sitting in the pleather chairs in the coffee shop reading book after book, because I didn't have enough money to buy any. Now Borders has gone out of business, and the store is a TK Maxx. And I have more books on my kindle than I will ever be able to read. When was the last time I read an actual real book? Had the tactile experience of turning pages? I resolve; I shall follow the Cambridge University Press sign, and buy an intellectual book.

The train lurches to a stop quickly, and the doors swing open. I grab my bag, my breakfast rubbish, and step off onto the platform. There aren't many other people getting off the train with me.

Cambridge on a wet Saturday afternoon doesn't seem like the most appealing destination, I suppose.

I walk towards the exit, and pass an AMT Espresso cart with a board that says, "warm up with a hot chocolate!" I look out at the rain that's still threatening to come pouring down and think that it's a good idea; and anyway, it's a literal sign, and I'm following signs. I join the queue, and order my hot chocolate. When the barista asks me if I want whipped cream, I agree to it. Hey, life is too short to not have cream on hot chocolate.

I make my way through the gates, and for a moment I wonder how I'll find a place to stay if I keep my promise to Sophie not to turn on my phone. How will I research places, check yelp reviews, and book them? Then I notice an advertising board on the wall next to the Marks and Spencer, and see some signs. One, a simple index card handwritten (in purple ink!) advertises "cozy rooms for tourists or students; daily, weekly, or monthly rates. Reasonable prices, lots of amenities, full English breakfast, five minute walk from the city centre." Well, that sounds about perfect to me.

There's a number on the bottom, and so I grab a pound coin out of my wallet and go to the phone box. When was the last time I touched a public phone, I wonder? Somewhere around 2001? For a moment I'm a little grossed out, wondering who else touched or threw up on it before me, and I am tempted to wipe it down with an antibacterial wipe. But then I realize how idiotic that sounds; after all, until I was out of college I never had a cell phone. I must have used public phones. And besides, I read that cell phones are some of the filthiest things we ever touch.

The phone rings, and an older woman answers with a simple "hello."

"Hello, is this the number for the bed and breakfast?"

"Oh yes, of course, it is. How can I help?"

"Would you happen to have a room tonight? Only, I'm just at the station and saw your sign and the cozy element seemed appealing on a day like today."

"Oh of course! I'm Eleanor, by the way. I'll have my husband Thomas come and collect you, all right?"

"That would be perfect!" I say with a smile and hang up.

Well, that was easy, and my phone is still off.

I stand at the doorway looking out at the bus stop, and feeling smug. This whole thing of following signs has worked wonders for me so far. I have a steaming cup of hot chocolate and a nice ride coming to take me to a cozy home where I shall rest and recharge. In a historic city that I've always wanted to see properly. Perhaps this is the start of me actually becoming an adult and putting the period of sordid messiness and terrible behavior behind me. Really healing from my past mistakes, and not just numbing myself with distractions and addictions. I can actually feel myself physically letting go of the recent me, and letting the well behaved Natasha back in. The one who somehow got lost in the rat race after the trauma of life knocked her out. Who started taking solace in alcohol and strangers in dark rooms with loud music.

Not to downplay the severity of my issues, I think. I'm going to need some help to get through this. If I really want to turn my life around, maybe I need some kind of coach or sponsor. For a moment I consider AA. I mean, really, if I am serious about this, having that support network might be in my best interest. I'm mulling this over, sipping my warm drink, when I see an older man pull up to the station and look around at the various groups of people, moving from one group to the next.

Finally his eyes settle on me, and he gives me a wave, rolls down the window, and yells, "Natasha?" I nod, and he immediately jumps out into the rain and grabs my bag from me before I can even realize what's happening.

"I'm Thomas," he explains. "Eleanor sent me down to collect you. Welcome to Cambridge. Here on holiday?" He talks a mile a minute, and I laugh as I watch him animatedly turn around in the station and head towards town. "You'll have to go punting, if you've never been before, though I suppose it's not the best weather for it. How long are you staying? Maybe it will improve. See the sights. Shopping along King's Parade, I expect?"

I smile at Thomas's energy. He's about 65, with graying hair, and a face that's framed on top with his laugh lines. I like him immediately, despite the fact that he's kind of making my headache worse. I wish I had his energy now. I hope I have it when I'm his age.

"Yes, I live in London, and I'm just up for the weekend."

"American are you?"

"Well, yes, but I live here now. In London."

"London is a beautiful city," he says. "But I do love America. At least the short trips we've taken."

He turns off towards Parker's Piece and then a row of terraced houses just on the other side of the green. "Here we are," he says. "Eleanor was just making sure your room was ready. We're giving you the gabled room. It has a window seat. Perfect for looking out at the rain."

"I'm sure it's lovely," I respond, and I actually am sure. The home is a normal terraced house; nothing special on the outside. But it feels so welcoming, and when I see Eleanor appear at the doorway, I feel as if I have met my long lost grandmother.

"Oh, dear, it's so wet out here. I've just made a pot of chamomile tea. Come on in, and we'll get you settled in."

We hug, I apologize for being wet and getting her soaked, she takes my coat and hands me a mug, all in a flash. Before I know it I'm seated on the couch in front of a fireplace, getting to know my new host over a plate of dark chocolate McVitie's. Today is turning out way more sugary and greasy than I ever intended, but I won't turn it down.

When Eleanor asks me what brings me to Cambridge for the weekend, I am surprisingly honest with her. "I had a bit too much of a party last night," I say.

"Young people do get up to some surprising things on Halloween," she says by way of acknowledgement and understanding.

"Indeed. Well, there are some photos."

"Honestly, these cell phones with their cameras and everything. No one can be stupid any longer," she exclaims. "Everything goes on tweetbook."

"Right, well, that's what happened to me. And I actually have a pretty high profile job in publishing. So it - the photo - somehow wound up on an internet gossip site. And now my boss wants to see me in approximately," I look at my watch, "43 hours."

"So you decided to get out of London to clear your head."

"At the advice of the head of publicity and PR for our company, yes."

"Oh dear girl, you've come to the right place! We will make things very relaxing for you. If you'd like a warm bath, we can get it running. We don't have any other guests at the moment, so we are fully available to pamper you."

I have fallen in love with this woman! She does hand me a contract with the price, and I cringe a little when I remember I'm trying to be frugal in case I'm sacked. But it's so near to the center of town and I can walk everywhere, so I think that the savings on cabs will make up for the cost. And anyway, the pampering is priceless.

I take Eleanor up on her offer of a bath, still feeling quite grimy after last night. The tub is an enormous old fashioned one that could easily fit three of me. Before I know it, my bag is dropped in my room, and I'm immersed in the hot sudsy water, looking out of the window at the homes and parks while drinking the hot tea. Eleanor had a spare Look magazine ("for the other visitors," she explained, blushing) and brings me a plate of McVitie's. For a moment I suppose that life truly can't get much better than this. I close my eyes and nap for what seems like only a few moments until I wake up in cold water and realize I've been napping for almost half an hour. Right. It's now very nearly 3pm, and there's more I want to do with my day before the inevitable darkness settles in.

I get up and dressed in a rush, grab my bag, bid a quick goodbye to Eleanor and Thomas, who are encouraging me in my desire to go see the sights ("Definitely try to go to choral Evensong at Kings - just heavenly! Wonderful for clearing your mind!" Thomas shouts at me, grinning), and walk over to the old center of town. My first stop is going to be the Cambridge University Press bookstore to pick up an intellectual book.

But as I'm walking past the ancient pathways towards the colleges, I pass a WH Smith and the fact dawns on me that I really should start journaling. Everyone I know seems to swear by journaling or meditating on the page, or whatever they call it. I wonder if it would work for me? Help me sort out and clarify some of the things that I'm trying to work through. I mean, it certainly couldn't hurt, right? I quickly go in and pick out a nice narrow-ruled notebook, and grab a pack of pens while I'm at it. I always seem to be running out of pens. I'm going to sit in the Cafe Nero with the intellectual book I'm about to purchase, and then journal how I'm feeling. I can just picture the quiet night I'll be having, and while it's a change from what my habit has been, the change seems to be from bad habits to good, so I can only embrace it.

Just as I'm leaving WH Smith with my lovely notebook and pens tucked into my bag, I see someone in the market square handing out flyers for the Evensong service at King's that Thomas mentioned. It occurs to me that it is All Saint's Day, the day after Halloween, a day to honor and remember the lives of the saints. There's also every chance that some of the spirits who came out to play during Halloween haven't quite found their way back into the underworld yet. It seems like an interesting thing to do with my time to go to the Evensong service. It's 3:20. I can still nip into the bookstore and then get to King's I think.

The Cambridge University Press bookstore is on the corner of the main parade where there are tiny alleyways that lead to the river, and a narrow thoroughfare with tiny cafes, shops, candy stores, and a wonderful classical music CD store, Heffer's, that I remember passing once on a way to a meeting at with an author at Trinity. I remember thinking that I really needed to come check it out and encourage my intellect again. Perhaps tomorrow I'll visit and do some thinking while listening to music. Maybe something choral. Early music.

I'm going to buy something scholarly, not thinking too much about it, picking the first thing that appeals to me without worrying that it looks too intellectual or some other nonsense like that. The title that jumps out at me is called "Banking in Crisis, the Rise and Fall of British Banking Stability, 1800 to the Present," by John D Turner, which looks dry and very intellectual, and costs a hefty twenty quid. But it jumped out at me, and so I choose it. I'm not really sure that I'll make it through the entire thing, but it will be a good exercise to start to read something that is out of my comfort zone. I pay for the book, push it into my bulging bag, and then run into the main King's entrance, stopping to collect myself as I walk into the ancient Chapel with quiet respect.

CHAPTER THREE

In Which Something Very Strange Happens

Instantly I feel transformed into someone else in a different place in time. This Chapel, which was built 600 years ago, invites people to become something greater and more connected to Source or God than they have been. God knows I haven't been very close to him/her/it in the past five years. I haven't really known what to say, really. Though I suppose that's silly. I've always believed that God is part of everything and everyone, so surely It has been with me even during the most recent crises?

The vaulted ceiling with the delicate intricate stonework reaching up to the sky, the arches, quiet hushed tones, and my footsteps sounding on the ancient stone; all create a certain sacred solemnity, knowing that you are walking on stone that scholars and theologians have walked on for six hundred years. This is why I moved to England all those years ago. This connection to history, to the people who came before me, to their stories; the ability to touch and live with their buildings, and to share part of their lives. I walk underneath the organ into the main choir area, and I wonder again how things got to the point that my mother has to see an instagrammed picture of me with a stripper and drugs. Can I ever get back to where I was?

I remember that I'm not going to think too much. Rather, I'm going to simply sit in silence, quiet my thoughts, and wait for the answers to come to me. I trust that they will. Sitting down in the choir stall on the very end nearest to the Rubens Adoration of the Magi altarpiece, I sigh in appreciation that these buildings, this artwork, this place of history and magic is still freely available to me, miserable offender that I am. I put my head down and am moved to talk to the ether.

"God, I seriously screwed up. But I'm sure you know that, right? It's bad, God. Like, really really bad. This recent episode is just the latest in the String of Messiness. But you already know that, right? I'm not entirely sure that I can fix this. But they say that nothing is beyond you, so I have to trust that you can help me. I really want to make it better. I want to stop acting like a drunk idiot. I want to value myself the way I know you value me. I want to love myself the way I know you love me. I want to start following my dreams again. Please help me."

Just then the choir begins to sing the chant and enter into the stalls with the procession of priests and clergy. It's a special service because of the All Saint's holiday, but the music, rather than being somber the way it would be expected, is joyous. A promise of Christ the Redeemer to His chosen people to walk with us even through the valley of the shadow of death.

The candles are flickering from the chandeliers high above, and electric lit tapers are on the choir stalls and around the rest of the building. But even still, with the oncoming early darkness and the rainy weather, it is dreary and haunting. There are shadows dancing around on the vaulted ceiling, which is so delicate that it looks like a little lace doily is miraculously holding up a ceiling on an enormous Chapel as if by accident. The stained windows are dark as there is so little light outside to illuminate them, but with the candles you can make out a few colors here and there.

The entire Chapel beyond the choir seems empty, and rather lonely, like there are monks scribbling on vellum parchments somewhere straining their eyes and wishing that they could come be part of the music making as well, but the manuscripts won't copy themselves.

I am feeling so moved by the entire experience that I begin to feel tears welling up inside of me. I have become so lost, and I'm present to it on a deeper level than I have been until now. I have to trust that there is a way back, and being here is going to help me find it. This is what I always craved when I moved to England. Music and history merging together with God and the universe like the way it does here. I used to go to services at Westminster Abbey after work during the week, and every Sunday. I'd smugly walk past the tourists and say, "I'm here for the service," to the usher whose job it was to ensure that the other Americans with high socks and giant bellies stayed outside the grounds, and only those who were properly prepared to pray for an hour would be allowed in.

The choir begins a contemporary piece, the O Magnum Mysterium by Morten Lauridsen, which I remember hearing once on ClassicFM. I thought it was beautiful at the time, but here, in this setting, words don't go far enough. It's heavenly. Sublime. It starts off so softly I almost have to strain to listen, a piece of liturgy usually sung at Christmas, The Great Mystery, to celebrate the mystery of Christ's arrival in a manger, and the Blessed Virgin and all of the manger animals who got to be part of the miraculous birth. The quiet of the opening chords brings me back to the present, the hard wood of the stalls beneath me, the stone under my feet, the candles in front of me, and for a moment I feel like perhaps my prayer is being answered, perhaps I can be close to this special world again. Maybe I can find peace and stop hiding from my past, and my shame.

The music reaches a crescendo as I am staring up at the ceiling, tears welling up in my eyes, thinking about where my life has gone. Blessed is the Virgin whose womb was worthy of bearing Christ the lord, they sing, in Latin. My womb doesn't feel very worthy these days, and just thinking about it makes me feel dizzy. Suddenly though I really am feeling faint. The choir is still singing, but things are spinning around me, very slowly at first, as if the room has just lost its balance and is swaying, but then it picks up, quickly, and I am literally watching King's College Chapel as if I'm on one of those teacup rides at the fair, with everything just swirling around me.

I take a deep breath and chalk it up to my hangover. I hold my bag on my lap, and lean over it, trying to put my head down like in a brace position, feeling my new notebook and scholarly economics book jut out and poke my belly. I barely register it though since I am now feeling incredibly dizzy and lightheaded, and it gets even worse when I close my eyes. I open them back up, but then all of a sudden the room is filled with shadows and dancing figures that no one else seems to see but me, and then there is blackness in my peripheral vision, and I'm feeling clammy and cold and sweaty all at the same time, and my heart starts to somehow beat faster and slower at the same time, and I'm swaying in my seat. This can't be just an effect of the music, though I've heard that Morten Lauridsen is brilliant.

For a moment I wonder if I made myself so sick last night that I'm going to pass out, and then I see an instant flash of light followed by overwhelming darkness.

CHAPTER FOUR

In Matthew's Rooms

I open my eyes, still clutching my bag, and there are men all around me, fanning me, talking to me, asking me who I am and what happened. They look like the choristers in gowns, and I am instantly embarrassed for the fact that I seem to have caused the entire service to stop. Yet another thing to add to the growing list of embarrassing things I'm doing. Pretty soon this is going to go on some Cambridge blog, and Sophie will have yet another crisis of mine that she needs to solve. I can't even get out of London properly. I take a minute to feel around and make sure no one has nicked my bag. Nope, I can feel my nice new thick economics book poking me in the ribs. Convenient, that is.

"My lady, please, let us know that you are well?" I look up into the face of one of the choral scholars, only he doesn't really look like a choral scholar. He's a bit old, for one thing. Perhaps he's one of the priests I didn't notice before. I sit up, clutching my bag to my chest, and look around. I notice three things. First, the lighting is all different than it was just a second ago when I passed out. The shadows are darker and more sinister looking. Second, the Rubens painting is gone from the altar. And finally, there is no one here who was just here. And almost everyone who is here is dressed like a chorister. And there are only two men not dressed as choristers here. And they both appear to be wearing burlap sacks.

I straighten up, feeling a bit woozy and dizzy, rub my eyes, and the face of a young man sitting to my right comes into focus. God, he smells. Like, seriously stinks. But he has kind eyes that appear worried about me, and when I look at him he smiles.

"Brother Edward, it appears that the lady is well," he says to the other older man.

"You may call her a lady, Brother Matthew, but I've no proof of that. She could be a heretic for all we know."

Hang on. What the? What the hell just happened to me?

The one called Matthew stands up in front of me, seeming to protect me. "We should not use such language when we do not have all the facts. It could be damaging, and we ought to be a bit more prudent before making accusations of such a strong nature. Brother Edward, I shall take responsibility for questioning her, and shall ensure that the truth of what just happened comes out. After all, it could be a miracle, and we would want to record and celebrate it. For now, please take the others and leave us in peace. It would be best if you didn't speak about this to any others not present. I know that asking you not to say anything would be asking for a miracle that even the Holy Spirit Himself would struggle to perform, but please be judicious with your tongue."

The one called Edward seems to turn reluctantly, and continuously looks back at me as if he's missing something. But he walks out the side door, with the rest of the crew following him.

"Madam, you must excuse his outburst. We do not see many females here, and the ones we do see are not dressed such as yourself."

I can only stare at him open mouthed. It's like I'm rendered mute. Or dumb. Or something.

"Come," he says, reaching his hand down for me, where I'm still sitting, clutching my bag. "We will go into my rooms, you will have some ale, and then you will tell me who you are, and how you came to be on the floor of our Chapel."

If only I could. Even ale couldn't solve this mystery, I think.

I follow him through the Chapel in a daze, and out the side door Edward had just exited. We turn left into a long hallway with wooden doors, behind which are probably the rooms and offices of the people involved in the college Chapel. I've never been in this part of the King's Chapel before, and I can't help being curious, looking around. Though there isn't that much to see in truth, since it's so dark. Matthew's small candle doesn't provide much light, and I keep looking down at my feet to make sure I'm not tripping over something, waiting for my eyes to adjust.

At the end of the hallway, Matthew opens a door and ushers me into what appears to be his study. There is a desk, a few volumes of parchment, some chairs, and blessedly, a fireplace. I hadn't realized how cold it is. It's still raining outside, I note. Of course it is. I'm still in England, obviously.

The thought occurs to me that perhaps I'm dreaming? Perhaps I fell asleep during the Evensong service, and this is all an elaborate game my subconscious is playing on me. Maybe I'll be given the best route forward for my meeting with Howard in this dream. I try to remind myself to remember the dream when I wake up, in case something really good happens.

Matthew invites me to sit down on a hard wooden chair by the fire, and he brings over a tanker of warm liquid - the aforementioned ale, I suppose. There's also a hunk of bread and what appears to be moldy cheese.

"Here, eat a bit. Then we'll talk."

I take a sip of the liquid, cough, and want to spit it out immediately. But Matthew has been kind up until now, and I'm not completely without manners. I pick at the bread and cheese, doing my best to eat it since Matthew is sitting in the chair opposite me; and recognizing that there must be hungry people here as well, and this cheese, moldy though it is, can't be cheap.

Finally I look over at Matthew. "Sir, thank you for your kindness. But I really don't know what to tell you," I say. "I have no idea what just happened. I was at Evensong service, and then I felt dizzy, and the world just went black. When I woke up it was with the other man looking at me."

Matthew looked confused. "Evensong? What is an Evensong service?"

"You know, the evening prayer."

"Vespers?" He looks genuinely confused.

"No, Evensong."

"But women aren't allowed at Vespers. It's only for Brothers and lay men." He seems to have latched on to me being at Vespers, so I'll go with that. "Did you sneak in, dressed as you are like a man, though clearly a foreign one?"

Hey, don't knock my jeans, mister. These are expensive.

"Madam, here is the situation, and I will be blunt. You were found in the private Chapel with a giant sack," he points to my bag, "very near to the altarpieces and reliquary. And you are clearly disguised as a man, though you are a woman. The penalty for stealing from the church is to be flayed alive. Edward just threatened to call you a heretic. You are in a precarious situation. I have custody of your person now, and I will do everything I can to help you if you are innocent of that of which you may be accused, but you must be honest with me."

Oh shit. This just turned into dangerous territory very quickly. Howard seems like a walk in the park compared to being flayed alive.

I sigh.

"Ok, look, Sir Matthew,"

"Brother Matthew," he corrects me.

"Ok, Brother Matthew. I don't know how, or why, or anything like that, but somehow I've come here, and you have to believe me there's not any kind of dark magic or witchcraft or anything like that going on here. My name is Natasha Delancourt. I come from the year 2015. I am the editor in chief at a publishing company in London called Court Magician. Evensong service came from Cranmer's Book of Common Prayer, I think. So if you're still talking about Vespers, well, I don't know. I'm clearly still in Cambridge, but somehow I seem to have...I don't know...wound up in another time?"

Matthew is hung up on one name. "Cranmer? I know of Cranmer. He was brought to power during the Boleyn marriage."

The wheels in my brain start turning. My medieval history degree might come in useful after all. I'd like to throw that in the faces of all the,"liberal arts are useless," naysayers. "Ok, so I'm somewhere around the mid 1500's here?" I'm wracking my brain, trying to remember things I knew like the back of my hand at one point.

"Madam, it is the year of our Lord 1539."

And I want to faint again.

Instead, I put my head in my hands, and lean over taking deep breaths. This is really not good. It's starting to sink in for me that I have done something that Stephen Hawking and the people who watch Through the Wormhole would be insanely jealous of.

I seem to have traveled in time.

We are both silent for a moment.

Then Matthew asks, "have you anything you can show me that could prove that you are from the time and place you say?"

Ah! My bag! My bag must be full of things that can show him. Please God, please let the things I packed still be there. Please let them have made whatever journey it is I made with me. I open my bag hesitantly, not sure what I'm going to find inside. But there's my new economics book, as I thought I felt it earlier! I pull it out and flip through the pages. Brother Matthew stares at me curiously.

"But all of those printed pages. You can read? And what material is that?"

"Oh, paper. Made of wood pulp. You won't see it, I'm afraid. It comes about during the Industrial Revolution, I think."

He looks curiously at me.

"Like three hundred years from now."

His eyes light up when I show him the copyright page, and he crosses himself.

"Dear God, you speak the truth. You do come from a different time. But you coming here must be a miracle! You must have some kind of truth that God wants you to share with us. Perhaps it's about the new teachings and the Lutherans in Germany."

Again, not so good. I remember learning about Bloody Mary and Foxe's Book of Martyrs, and I know that speaking out about religion right now is not a good idea. And I'm starting to get my spinning head around the idea that I've gone back in time some 500 years, and I might actually be stuck here. If that's what's going to happen, I need to plan. And I don't plan on becoming some kind of visionary mystic Hildegard of Bingen type of person. I want to lay low and gather my thoughts before anything else happens. I laugh thinking that Sophie would probably tell me to go away for the weekend and get out of London. Well, I left London, and here I am, stuck in a monastic college full of men, and one of them threatened to call me a heretic about 20 minutes ago.

I take a deep breath.

"Brother Matthew. Let me talk to you - confidentially, if I may?"

He nods, looking curious and excited, leaning forward to see what wisdom the potential prophet might impart.

"Look, I can show you an entire bag of artifacts from 2015. Like my cell phone. Your head will spin with it all, I promise you. And bubblegum. Here, have a piece," he takes a piece of my Extra gum and looks at it like it might bite, following my lead when I put a piece in my mouth. Then he looks pleased and starts chewing in earnest, and smiles at me. " And look at this blank paper - it cost me less than a mug of ale costs. And check out these pens."

Matthew, clearly a scholar, about loses it over the paper and pens. He spends a good ten minutes writing his name on the blank paper, as well as some Bible verses.

"But here's the thing, Brother Matthew," I say, taking back the pen and paper to his clear dismay. I'm not about to hand over all the goods this soon. I might need them for bargaining chips later. See, I can still think strategically.

"In about 15 years, things are going to get really bad for religious prophets here. There's an alcoholic drink named after Princess Mary because of what she's remembered for: Bloody Mary." Mathew looks at me aghast. "There's also a famous book of martyrs that came out of England during Mary's reign."

Matthew stares dejectedly down at his hands. "It's such a difficult time now, with all the new thinking. It's hard to know which way is up."

"Oh, I totally get it. But the point is, I'm not really a fan of being a martyr."

"Of course. But if you'll allow me to be honest..."

"Absolutely. I'd love it."

"Word of this is going to get around. I'm trying to think of how best to protect you. And truly, for all we know, you could have been sent here by God. Surely you must know some great Truths about us all, about humanity that you could impart to our great benefit."

I remember now that life really isn't the same way it was when I left this morning. I can't simply get on a train and get back to London. A woman traveling by herself would be in great danger here, no matter what her status. I'm going to need protection. Matthew could maybe protect me, if I could give him something in return. He wants great truths? I'll give him some great truths. I dig into my bag for this morning's Guardian.

"Brother Matthew, this is a newspaper. It reports on the news and what's happening in the world."

Matthew leans forward eagerly.

"You will notice that there are stories of war, and murder, and vice, and fornication, and all of the great sins of the world, the same way there are vices and murders and thefts and wars today." Matthew grabs the paper and starts to look at it. The pictures especially amaze him. I can only imagine what sort of excitement and fear he must be experiencing. Like if I suddenly showed up at Hogwarts from King's Cross.

"Humanity hasn't changed that much, Brother Matthew. England has become more of a secular society, to its credit, I think. Too many people are going to be killed in the next hundred years especially, in the name of Truth. Each group believes that theirs is the only Truth, and if everyone doesn't follow it they'll go to hell, so they should be burned for heresy. England will waffle back and forth between Protestant and Catholic. When one group gets into power, they'll kill the other group. It's horrible and shameful. As time goes on, people become more tolerant of each other and different religions. At least in theory. There are still wars where one group wants to kill the other for being different. But in general, people in England aren't killed for their religious beliefs any longer. There are even Muslims and Jewish people living here quite peacefully."

Matthew is hanging on every word of mine, drinking in this knowledge of the future.

"I have often pondered the futility of killing people when we should be a beacon of Christ's love," he says quietly. "But there is such fear right now. Our way of life is being threatened. You were in Cambridge, in this very Chapel, so the college still exists in the future? We haven't been completely wiped out?"

"Cambridge is one of the great universities in the world," I say. "Tourists come here from all parts of the world to visit, and to sit in this Chapel. Services are packed every day. People are turned away. I can assure you, Cambridge in general, and King's in particular is very healthy in the future. See the book I showed you before? Cambridge University Press. One of the premiere scholarly presses in the world."

"That's a relief at least," he responds.

We sit in silence for a few moments. I watch the fire flickering, and take in the gloominess of my surroundings, the old rushes on the floor, the dim candlelight. I'm starting to wonder where I'm going to sleep tonight. As if reading my mind, Matthew interrupts the silence.

"There is a woman, out in the fens," he starts quietly.

I lean forward. If this is a plan, I want in.

"She has a reputation as...well, not as part of the community. She is a healer. The brothers and scholars here are afraid of her, but I have always found her to be quite gentle. She lives on her own, and people go to her when they feel that physicians can't help them. Or if they can't afford physicians."

I can't wait to tell Matthew about the fact that bloodletting is totally bogus.

"I believe she may be able to help you. At least she can keep you safe while we figure out a plan. It is night soon. We can bundle up and row out to her. I will speak with her for you. She trusts me. We...well, we trust each other. She will take care of you until we can devise a plan of what to do next." I can see the tenderness welling up in Matthew as he looks away from me. I do believe he might have a crush on this woman. Ahh, how romantic. Unrequited love. I'm suddenly feeling very soft on Matthew.

"Hey Matthew," I say. He looks up at me. "You know, human beings have gone to the moon. It's pretty amazing."

"Truly? To the moon?"

"Yep. Men have walked on the moon and brought back rocks and soil."

"What a magnificent time in which you live. Surely you thank God every day for this peace and these inventions?"

"I should, but I admit that I do not. Not every day. But being here...if I never get back there... I will."

CHAPTER FIVE

Alice

Matthew decides that it's best for us to travel in complete darkness so he can safely transport me to the mysterious benefactor's home, and during the wait he looks at my books, the newspaper, and other magnificent things like post-it notes. I sip some more of the ale, which is slowly growing on me, and try to cover up the fact that my stomach is growling. I do not want to be offered more of the moldy cheese.

Finally he thinks it safe to bundle me up in a cloak, grab a candle, and lead me back through the shadows and the menacing looking stained glass windows to the front door. We jog down to the river, a familiar feeling since I've done it before when visiting in my own time, and there are several boats docked at a small wharf jutting into the narrow river. The moon is out, and I can see the water reflected all around me. In a hundred years this landscape would look so different, as progress was made in draining the fens and reclaiming the useable farmland. But now, it's still swamp and full of eels and other nasty creatures. I sit in the boat, hugging my bag to me, and Matthew uses the pole to punt us through the water. I've gone punting several times with friends or family when they would come to visit, but it looks very different now with many of the famous colleges not even in existence yet.

The light of the moon is shining on the water, and the stars are so much brighter than I could ever imagine. I can see entire galaxies out there. No wonder people were so amazed by the heavens. These days you're lucky if you can see the Big Dipper on the Hampstead Heath because of all the city lights.

I huddle in the bottom of the boat, keeping my head down in case we are seen. We want as few people as possible to know about my arrival. Edward has already seen me, and he seems to be the college gossip. I will have to think of a way to make sure that the rumors he spreads have no truth to them.

"Matthew," I whisper.

"Yes?" he says, sounding like he's concentrating. I can imagine punting would be difficult at night.

"Do I have reason to fear Edward?"

He is silent for a moment. Then, "I will tell him something that will satisfy him for now. I believe your story, and I want you to be safe. I want us to learn from you. At least I want to learn from you myself. The moon... unbelievable. If Edward gets people stirred up, he'll be writing to his friend on the privy council next and you'll be summoned to London. That wouldn't turn out in your favor. Either you'd be sentenced as a heretic, or you'd go to Bedlam. Neither is a good choice for an innocent messenger of God."

Well, I'm not so innocent, I think, remembering the whole reason this visit to Cambridge started.

Matthew seems to read my mind. "My lady, Natasha, what brought you to our college today?" he asks. We are out of the main part of town now, and can talk more freely. It's so quiet, I think. There are no planes. No drunk people screaming at a football match on the tv. No loud music coming from anywhere. Just the sound of the pole and the boat slicing through the water. Some crickets.

"I got into a bit of trouble in London at a Halloween party," I say. "I wanted to get away for a bit and think about how to handle it."

"But surely it's a long journey?"

"Only an hour by train," I respond. "Oh, trains. Another product of the industrial revolution. Large carriages that can carry many hundreds of people great distances at speeds that are unbelievably fast. You can journey from London to York in just 2 hours on a fast train."

"What a miracle!" Matthew exclaims loudly, and then lowers his voice again. "You must be in awe of the pace at which you can travel."

"Well, I mean, it's been around my entire life, and my parents' lives, so it's not like it's that new. You kind of take it for granted now. You know, human beings can fly, too. You can fly from London to Rome in three hours in a large flying carriage. That's really only been around for about sixty years or so by the time I'm alive, so it's still something that my parents, for example, are in awe of."

"God in heaven, the glories and mercies that are poured into Your Creation. Flying!" Matthew breathes.

I get a pang thinking about my parents. Will I ever see them again? And then my head starts to spin again, because really, what will they think happened to me? What's happened to future me? Like, right this moment, am I still laying on the floor in King's? Did I just disappear?

"Well, you wanted to get away and think about things, and God, as usual, has provided a way," Matthew chuckles.

We sit in a pleasant and companionable silence for about twenty minutes more while Matthew punts us through the swampland. Then we come to a small island on which stand about

15 small shacks, a small church, and a fenced in area with livestock, who all appear to be sleeping.

Matthew pulls the boat up onto the land and then helps me out and up to a small hut on the edge. There is an herb garden at the side, and a lovely thatched roof, with smoke puffing out of a small hole cut in the center.

He knocks very quietly on the door. "This is Alice's house," he whispers.

The door opens, and from the dim light inside I can make out the figure of a woman who is a few years younger than me. She is thin and looks tired, but I can see the same friendly sparkle in her eyes as I saw in Matthew's. She smiles at him. "Matthew," she sighs quietly.

Then she sees me. "Jesu, what have you brought me?

"May we enter?"

"Yes, of course," and the door opens further, though slightly reluctantly, and she gestures to have us enter.

Alice looks to be in her mid-twenties, about the same age as Matthew, with gentle features. Her light brown hair is swept up in a braid that is wrapped around her head, and her blue eyes are alert as she beckons us inside. Her clothing is old and stained, but her home is comfortable enough with a pallet bed next to the open fire, a small table. I see a shelf full of crushed herbs, and what appear to be various creams and potions. She seems to be the resident healer, and she carries herself with a certain grace and wisdom, though she still looks wary of me. She smiles at me somewhat cautiously, taking in my odd appearance.

"Alice," Matthew begins, sitting down on a stool by the fire. "This is Natasha of Delancourt. She showed up in the Chapel today. She has shown me proof which I believe is authentic that she has come to us from another place...and another time."

Alice looks at me and at first she appears confused by what Matthew has just said. I look back sheepishly and shrug my shoulders, then I watch as she comprehends it. Her face blanches, then she sits down on the other stool.

"But how can that be? What proof?"

"She has shown me things from the future. She comes from the year 2015, nearly five centuries in the future. She will show them to you as well."

"God in heaven!" comes out the exclamation, as Alice crosses herself.

Matthew gestures to me, and I sit down at their feet by the fire.

"Show her the book," he instructs me.

I pull it out, never imagining that I would be so grateful for an economics book.

Alice takes it and holds it in her hands, looking at it suspiciously, but reverently.

"This material that the words are printed on... what is it?"

"It's paper," I respond, thinking it curious that both she and Matthew asked that right away.

"It was invented about 300 years or so from now, I think. Here," I lean over and start to thumb through the pages to get to the copyright date. "the copyright page has the date on it."

She brings it closer to her eyes and takes it in, mumbling, "whatever a copyright may be."

"It's true," she whispers. "But how?" she looks at Matthew.

"I do not know," he responds. "Nor does she," he nods at me. "But somehow God has seen fit to have her come here, and I would like to take care of her until we can figure out what to do." A pause, then. "Edward has seen her."

"Oh no," she groans. "What will you tell him?"

"I will make something up about her being a pedlar or in need of hospitality or something. It will keep him quiet for a little while, at least."

She looks grim.

"And so you brought her to my home, so that when Edward finds out she is still here, he may have double the reason to curse my home?" She spits out the words, sounding bitter.

"Alice, I did not think of it that way, and he does not curse your home, I promise you that. I believed I could trust you to help me by helping her."

"You continue to put me in danger, bringing attention to my peculiar gifts and causing the scholars and brothers to hate and fear me."

"I know, I ask too much of you. You do me too much service. But the things she can tell us, the messages she may have... I would like to make sure she is safe, and I can think of no one more able to do that."

"Very well," she sighs, clearly knowing she was going to give in before the conversation even started. "Since you have brought her here already, without my permission or even doing me the courtesy of asking me...then it's probably time you leave her with me as well. I will make sure no harm comes to her."

"Thank you, Alice."

"You're welcome, Matthew," she says, reluctantly.

I watch them quietly quarrel and sense that there is much more feeling behind the polite words, and I wonder what the story is. Matthew glances over at me. "I knew Alice growing up. She's one of my oldest friends. You will be cared for here. I will come to see how you are faring soon."

And with that he reaches over and squeezes her hand, probably an illicit hand squeeze given that he is affiliated with the college, and he leaves. Then I am left alone with Alice, who is standing by the fire, staring at me.

CHAPTER SIX

Taking Stock

Alice doesn't say much at first, but she busies herself by making a small straw pallet on the floor for me, I suppose, and covering it with furs. It looks warm, and I realize for the first time how cold it is. She pours me some broth with vegetables in it, and then sits down next to me near the fire.

"I'm very grateful for your hospitality," I say feebly. It's clear that she doesn't particularly want me as a houseguest.

"If you are going to be here in my home, you may as well tell me your story," she responds.

"Do you want the short version, or the long one," I halfway joke.

"I have nowhere else to go, and seemingly neither do you, so I'll hear it all," is the answer.

And so I tell her, looking into the fire, trying to get it all straight in my head as I speak the words. The broth is warming me inside, and I feel safe here in this cozy home with this woman, though how I can feel that way is beyond me right now. But I tell her about my life in London in 2015. How I came with such high hopes and expectations for myself. And how it all went sour when I started drinking and partying, though I don't tell her the story of the pain I was numbing or what I was running away from. That wound is still too deep, and I fear that Alice would think her trust in me was misplaced if I told her about the baby that existed in me for such a short time, and my own guilt about my miscarriage, which I believe I must have caused from my uncertainty about whether to end the pregnancy.

I do mention how I was wasting away in clubs. And then the terrible night - was it just last night? - when everything really went wrong, and the pictures that were seen by so many, and my boss Howard, who is now so angry. How I came away to the countryside to get out of London and catch my breath, and how I thought I would turn over a new leaf, and become a better me. And then, how I went to Evensong service, felt so dizzy, and woke up five hundred years earlier.

She listened to me and interrupted me from time to time to remind me to eat my broth, and to ask a question, but for the most part she kept quiet and took it all in.

"Your clothing..." she started.

"yes?"

"May I touch it?"

I nod, and she reached out and stroked my clothing, picking at the cloth and examining the stitching. She was ridiculously excited about my jeans, boots, sweater and jacket, the latter of which I let her try on. When she slipped her arms into the downy jacket the look on her face was both puzzled and ecstatic. She didn't care so much about the fashion, but was fascinated by the textiles.

"You truly do come from another place. Fibers like this... I have never seen anything like it."

"Yep, that would be the Industrial Revolution again."

I tell her a bit about America, and where I come from in Los Angeles. I describe flying on a plane, in detail all the way down to TSA screenings. I tell her what London is like now, and how the fens have been drained, and how many colleges there are in

Cambridge. I feel very proud of all the talking I'm doing; it's good to get it all out, and she seems like a willing listener.

Then she sits back in the chair, looks at me, and starts to laugh.

"My God, Natasha. What a pile of trouble you are in, are you not?"

At that point I take out my phone. I've had it turned off all day, so there is still a full charge, and I half expect for messages to start popping up, until I realize they won't because there is no cell tower. Knowing that the search for a network can drain the battery, I immediately put it into airplane mode.

I am able to show her pictures of my friends, and of London. She recognized the Tower of London from when she had been to visit family there once, and is amazed that it's still standing, the building was already half a millennium old when she saw it. I show her pictures of Cambridge. And when I pass through pictures of my family I almost start to cry. I want to keep this phone forever with my pictures and my connection to them, but eventually it will lose its charge, and I won't be able to plug it back in.

Alice is, of course, stunned by everything I'm showing her. I would be too. Imagine someone showing up at your house and saying they're from 500 years in the future, and then showing you a bunch of weird devices that we haven't even thought of yet, and some of it is familiar because they show you places you know, but at the same time it's all different, and you can't really tell which way is up.

We talk into the middle of the night, almost morning. I want to turn the phone off to preserve the battery, and also to give Alice's brain a break, but before I do, I play some music for her. Oh God, how I will miss recorded music if I can't get back. I play her Beethoven, the 7th Symphony, a piece I've loved since before I can even remember. I tell her who Beethoven is, and she just stares at the phone, in the direction of the sounds she is hearing; and the fact that they can sound like they are being performed in the same room must blow her away.

Then I show her my ebook collection on my phone - if I am stuck here truly, I will grieve the loss of my ebooks...so many books I will never read...I can't think about it. But Alice takes it all in so quietly and calmly, and reads the print on the screen, amazed at what she's seeing, that I finally insist in turning the device off. She wonders whether everyone in my time has a device like mine, or just wealthy people? I tell her that even in a lot of countries where there is poverty, people still use phones like this to communicate. She is awestruck. Of course she is. Maybe I shouldn't have thrown so much at her so quickly.

Alice starts murmuring about going to sleep, since we've been talking for hours and we still need to get up early for church. I assume that I'll be sleeping on the pallet by the fire, so I head over to it and sit on top of the fur, which is scratchy and warm, and smells slightly of dampness. It's sad, I think, that I don't know what animal this belongs to. I suppose if I'm going to be here for a while, I'll become familiar enough with them eventually.

Feeling lonely and scared, I empty out the contents of my bag on the fur in front of me, and take stock of what I have.

- A wallet with approximately 80 pounds sterling, useless credit cards, an oyster card, a costa coffee rewards card, my passport, and some sentimental papers like club receipts and movie tickets.
- A bag of makeup which includes several lip glosses, powder, an eyeshadow palette, foundation, eyeliner and a mascara.
- A tub of Brazil Nut body butter from the Body Shop.

- Oh My God! A solar powered phone charger! I remember this now! It was still in my bag from the camping trip. A gift from Sophie I had brought along thinking I would be super prepared for spending time outside the city in the wilds of Cornwall. Oh praise the Lord! I check to make sure it fits both my phone and my iPad, and it does! I'm not sure how much I'll be able to use it in November in England, where the sun makes only a rare cameo appearance, but just knowing that I have this lifeline to my past means the world to me. Hurrah!

Feeling infinitely better about life, I continue to go through my belongings, emptying things out and shaking the bag to make sure I haven't missed a spare bobby pin. Who knows what will be important here?

- A tin of mints, and two packs of gum
- A granola bar
- Phone
- iPad
- Kindle (no charger, so that will be a shame)
- blank notebook
- eight pens
- economics book
- diary from WH Smith, leather, with entirely new refill for the new year, purchased in a fit of Planning Fever when a reminder popped up 3 weeks ago that it was time to buy refills. Post-it notes included.
- glasses
- pack of Nurofen
- pack of Rennies

- headphones
- a pair of jeans, 2 pairs of knickers, 2 pairs of socks, an extra bra, and a long sleeved black turtleneck, packed for tomorrow.
- nightgown
- newspaper

That's it. That's the contents of what is left of my entire life from before. I stare at it, and feel tears running down my cheeks. Alice, moving around putting things away, watches me. I unzip my Clarks walking boots and look at my socks. So incredibly comfortable, and so not practical for wearing here.

She brings me a mug of something warm.

"Drink this and you'll feel a little better. It's got some peppermint, some chamomile, and a bit of fennel."

Then she goes over to her small bed, which is really just a pallet like mine, but raised off the ground, and she goes to sleep. I also crawl into bed, but even though I'm exhausted, I'm still awake when the fire dies down. Eventually I drift off, though, welcoming the blackness and the abyss of sleep, where I can continue to live my normal life.

CHAPTER SEVEN

Church

It seems like I've only been asleep for five minutes when the sounds of the island village coming to life wake me up. I feel like it's early but Alice is already preparing breakfast. She sees me stirring, comes over to where I'm laying, and sits next to me.

"It's a fair day, and I'm going to the herb garden for a bit before church. I've been thinking what to tell people about who you are. I think I must say that you are a relative who has come to stay because your husband died in one of the wars in Scotland. You can wear my extra dress until we can get some cloth to make you one. The next Market in Cambridge is Thursday. We can take care of it then. Your name, Natasha - it won't really do. It sounds so foreign. We'll call you Margaret. No one can argue with a good strong name like Margaret."

She hands me a hunk of cheese, a crusty loaf of brown bread, and an onion. "Here's some food. I've laid the dress out on my bed. You can change, and then come out and join me. If anyone asks, you've arrived from London late yesterday. You were with a group of pilgrims who are on their way to Ely, and you traveled with them this far."

I nod, taking it all in. I'm suddenly Margaret. As if it's not bad enough that I'm away from home, from my own country and my own time period, now I'm not even myself any longer? But it makes sense. I don't think there are any Natasha's in this time period. I need to be a Margaret. I wonder if it will change my personality at all, wearing this new name to go with my new homespun dress.

I change into Alice's clothes, leaving my own underwear on - I do have limits - and I go out to join her once I've had my food. She shows me the different herbs she's picking out. We are going to make a poultice of St. John's wort, chamomile, fennel, and motherwort for a neighbor who has been having some depression issues. Well, Alice doesn't say depression. She calls it feeling black.

"You know, in my time, people still use these kinds of herbs for melancholy," I say. "Only we don't grow them ourselves. They're already ground up and put into tiny pills we get at the natural health store and swallow with water."

I take a moment to look around this little island on which there are a dozen or so homes, all with comfortable looking thatched roofs, gardens, and punting boats gathered at a small docking area. It's a clear day, with bright white puffy clouds. An unusual day for November. But it's lovely. There are birds singing, and everything is still.

A boat approaches with a fisherman who is catching eels. "Ho there Alice," he yells out to us, looking at me.

"Hallo John."

He nods to me.

"This is my cousin Margaret. She just arrived from London," she yells back.

"Welcome Margaret!" John the fisherman yells.

"Hallo John, thank you" I respond in kind.

He continues on his way and Margaret informs me that I'm going to have to work on my speech, or else people are going to be suspicious.

"You just don't sound like you're from London," she says.

"I'm not, I'm from Los Angeles," I agree.

"Yes, well, we're provincial up here, and we can recognize if someone is clearly not one of us."

I promise to work on it, and she gives me a small smile.

"I tend to be a bit guarded," she starts out. "Please don't think it has anything to do with you. People are often hard with me, and so I've become hard with them too."

I tell her about my meeting Brother Edward and she grimaces. "He hates me. He'd have me burned as a witch. I'm not a witch," she says looking at me. I nod. I understand. If I had lived during this time, I'm sure people would think I was a witch, too. Then the thought that people might indeed think I'm a witch, because I actually am living here now, chills me. I know enough about what they did to witches to know that would not be a good outcome.

"Matthew protects me," she says, smiling. "And the people here in our village do, too. Other than that, I try not to go into town much, and when I do, I stay away from the colleges. It's funny, though, they, the students and scholars often come to me. When they've no other choice."

"And I'm sure you treat them with love, right?"

"Of course I do. I suppose part of me hopes that they will start to see that I'm not evil."

"How did you get to this place of being such an outsider?" I want to know how such a vivacious young woman can wind up afraid and alone like this.

"Ahh," she seems to look inside of herself. "I made some poorly thought out choices when I was younger. Then I discovered that I had special abilities to heal people. And I realized that I got along better with animals than with people. Add that all up, and you've got a perfect combination for some people to mistrust me."

I'm grateful for the ability in our time to move easily and reinvent ourselves when things get really bad. Of course it's not always so easy - jobs don't generally travel - but it's so much easier for us now, where anonymity, even in the age of Facebook, can make moving and starting a new life possible. And even if we don't move, the pace of life moves so quickly that our mistakes are often forgotten so soon after they happen. The 24 hour news cycle ensures that there's always something new. Suddenly my meeting with Howard on Monday - if I ever get to Monday - seems so much less important. Hell, by Monday maybe Lindsay Lohan will have been arrested again, or Taylor Swift will be dating somebody new.

"What were the mistakes you made?" I ask, curiously.

"There was a child."

Ahhhh. A child is forever. Until it's not.

I note her use of the word "was," and it brings a small wave of sadness to me. I know the feeling, I think. But I stop myself. Mustn't go there. Not yet. I just can't think about it. Eventually I suppose I'll have to tell Alice about why I kept trying to run away. If I'm ever going to get to the other side of it myself, which, I'm beginning to suspect is part of why I'm here. But I'm only a day in. A day of a potential lifetime, which makes me shudder. No, for now, I just want to focus on her story.

"What happened?"

"She died as a babe. Not very surprising given the chill here in the fens. Many children die. There's a woman, Mary, down the road, she's lost 12 of her 14. And look at what happened to our own Queens Katherine and Anne. Even being Royal doesn't shield you from the risks of having children. But there was scandal. The father; well, we were never married, you see. He was in the church. So it was very...uncomfortable. When she died, some said it was for the best. Others accused me of doing it myself; first getting myself pregnant to somehow trap him, and then when it didn't work, ridding myself of her. They didn't know. And I don't have family nearby, so I was on my own without much protection. The things people said..."

We're silent for a moment. I know enough to know there aren't any words to help make her feel better.

"I'm sorry, Alice. People can be so hurtful. That doesn't change, I'm afraid."

She smiles at me sadly. "No? Humanity doesn't progress past that by the 21st century?"

I think about it for a minute.

"You know, I think we'd like to have. I think we wish we had. We make laws to protect people - anti-discrimination laws where you can't fire someone because of their religion or sex or because they're pregnant, for example." She looks impressed. "But yet somehow, Alice, we managed just thirty or so years before I was born to, as a species, create the most efficient systematic killing machines. And then terrorism started to take off."

I tell her quickly about the Holocaust, and the atomic bomb, September 11. Her expression turns to horror. "So you see, I think human nature must be mostly the same. I think perhaps we like to think that we've progressed and matured and somehow risen above ancient prejudices. But I don't think we have, really. Our base animal instincts must still be pretty intact."

She looks thoughtful.

"But it does seem as if you're trying."

"I think we are. It's really great that you can't be persecuted for your religion, for example. And people, in theory, get a fair trial. And people who are mentally ill don't go to Bedlam any longer. There are medicines, and better hospitals. I think we try to be understanding. We want to be understanding. But humanity can only progress so fast, I guess."

Just then a couple with several children of all shapes and sizes from the neighboring cottage come falling out in a pile.

"Are you going to church? Alice?"

She looks at me. "My cousin, Margaret, arrived last night. She's been traveling from London with a group of pilgrims on their way to Ely."

They all smile. Though the husband seems to look at me a bit suspiciously.

"Margaret, these are my neighbors, the Coopers."

I do my best to remember how I'm supposed to talk, and say, "pleasure."

Alice winces. "She's still got her accent from Cornwall," she says.

"Ahhh, Cornwall. I was raised there. What part are you from?" the husband asks. Suddenly my mind goes blank. I've spent plenty of long summer weekends in Cornwall, in Newquay and Penzance. But I have no idea the history of those places, and whether they were even around now. I mean surely there must have been towns there in the 16th century. But I just can't think of anything. And so I respond, "Actually, it's Somerset. Glastonbury." Because I know for a fact that Glastonbury has been around for a long time. King Arthur was supposedly buried there.

"The West Country certainly is beautiful," the husband says to me. "Surely does make Cambridgeshire look drab by comparison."

"And the rain doesn't help!" I laugh. "But I do like it here. The universities. The bend in the river outside Trinity college."

"Which college?"

Oh shit. Henry VIII founded Trinity. When? When when when did he found it? I can't remember.

"Oh, I mean Queen's." Queens was founded by Margaret of Anjou and Elizabeth Woodville. That's been around for a while.

"Yes, it's a lovely spot there," the wife says. "I do like to walk around there on market days sometimes."

But the husband is still looking at me curiously.

Alice steps in. "Yes, we'll be coming to church in just a minute. This one's a bit religious," she says, pointing at me.

Then when they're gone, "That wasn't good. He's a stonemason. Employed to work on the new college, only no one knows yet what it's to be called!"

"Well I'm sorry Alice. I'm sorry if I mixed up 1539 from 1546. It's all ancient to me!"

"It's ok. We can say one of the pilgrims told you. Pilgrims are good anonymous sources of information. Just make sure you do well in service today."

Just what I need, another test. Service. "Alice, what is this now? Protestant? Catholic? What kind of service is it?"

"Same old service as ever. I'm sure there are changes in the services in the big cities, and in the colleges, but for our small parish church, we haven't embraced any of them yet."

"Alice, I've never been to a Catholic service before. I won't know what to do."

Her eyes get huge. "I'm even considered a heathen, and even I know what to do in service. You grow up in it, no?" I shake my head. "Ok, just follow my lead."

And our quiet morning of introspection and intimate conversation ends as she runs inside to take her apron off and splash some cold water on her face. I follow suit, feeling grateful that I overpack and had my favorite tinted moisturizer in my bag, which seems to endlessly impress Alice. Then we walk over to the other side of the island to a small village parish church made of timbers rather than stone, with a thatched roof. It's a short walk, and a boy is singing something in Latin as we walk in. I stick close to Alice as she introduces me to a few people, and we slide onto a bench.

I expected a Catholic service to be steeped in incense and chanting, but this looks like something out of a Monty Python sketch. A bumbling priest comes in carrying a relic. It's Saint Wilifred's toenail, supposedly. And behind him comes the other priests carrying crosses and blowing around a tiny amount of incense, and singing chants out of key.

There are almost as many priests as there are worshippers. If you can call them that. Just like in many modern day churches, the men seem preoccupied. I see one of them betting on something with another. A child eats a lump of cheese, and then gives pieces of it to a rat sitting at his feet (I really want to interrupt and say something about the bubonic plague, but I keep my mouth shut).

Some of the women are gazing off into space. There aren't many windows, and the ones that are are actually open, not protected with any kind of fancy glazed window panes. They're just open to the November weather, though today it's sunny so I don't mind. But I don't think I'd enjoy a Christmas eve service here. The rushes on the floor stink, and I swear I can feel other rats and mice moving around inside of them. I do my best to keep my feet off the floor. Many of the children are running around. The entire place is dark and damp, but with weird shadows coming through the narrow windows.

The priests are chanting in Latin. No one understands anything. Because I've sung some choral music, I actually know a little bit of what they're saying in the chants, but everyone else looks completely uninterested. Then it comes time for the Communion, where the bread literally turns into the Body of Christ. People, thousands of them, will die in the next few decades because of the debate about transubstantiation - whether the bread really becomes the body, or whether it's just symbolic. I watch as the priests bless the stale and rat-nibbled wafers, and distribute the bread and wine to the people, who actually have no idea what kind of mystical ceremony they are taking part in, but are just doing it because it's how they've been raised.

I'm not the most religious person in the world, as my recent lapses in judgment will attest, but I firmly believe that if you're going to compel people to go to a service, you should at least tell them what's happening. Who they're worshipping and why, for example. These people clearly don't know much about the story of Jesus or the ceremony and hymns that they are singing. They are just going through the motions. No wonder the Protestants want to get the Bible in English, and services in English. This forced inaccessibility doesn't serve anyone's spirit.

And the stupid relics. We're supposed to go pray to and kiss Oswald's toenail or Peter's eyelash, or something else equally as ridiculous. This is just awful. Poor people who have rats in their thatch being forced to give money to these monks so they can parade around fake relics and transubstantiated bread. No wonder the Reformation was welcomed by so many people who were hungry for a faith they could actually understand. And why the establishment fought it so much.

These priests have a pretty sweet deal, I think. They just go around finding bits of bodies and calling them relics, say some stuff in Latin that no one understands (I bet they themselves don't even understand it much of the time) and offer up salvation. It almost makes me angry. Until I remember that there must be some good monks who are doing good work, caring for the poor and feeding the hungry. Surely they can't all be fat and stupid like these ones, with their hairy noses and greasy foreheads.

I think I might be a secret Protestant. Who knew? But I suppose I'd better be careful about whether I share that information. Like I told Matthew last night, I don't really fancy becoming a martyr, and the idea of being burned at the stake as a heretic is really not particularly appealing.

Just as the communion service is finishing, my thoughts, which have drifted so close to the textbook definition of heresy here, are interrupted by what seems to be the final show. A low whisper starts to run through the benches. The betting stops. Everyone, even the children, sit up straight and pay close attention. Alice's face looks grim, and she grasps my hand. She leans over and whispers to me, "I had hoped you wouldn't have to see this." I have no idea what I'm about to witness, but it scares me already.

Everyone seems to know when to turn around and look at the front entrance, where a young boy is leading a woman, literally leading her with a piece of old cloth around her neck. She looks miserable, but everyone else looks really happy and excited. Laughter starts up, and then the jeering.

"Maybe next time you'll be able to keep her mouth shut yourself, eh Richard?" someone yells out. I notice a man in the front, probably in his early thirties, sitting with four children. All of them look pained. He puts his head down when the laughter really picks up.

At this point the woman, who is wearing only a dirty white shift and her hair loose hanging down to the middle of her back, has arrived at the front, and is facing away from us, towards the priest. Her youngest children start to cry, and that only makes people laugh harder.

"Learn from your mother's mistakes, girl," another man cries out. The woman in front turns and gives her husband and children a sad smile, and the man nods to her, seemingly sending her strength and resolve. The priest turns her head back to him.

"Anne, wife of Richard Bristol of the Fenland. You have been found guilty of talking too much, and of malicious gossip. And so, it is with prayers for your soul that you are able to use this time to find forgiveness and meditate on the wrongs of which you have been found guilty, that we now put you in the brank."

I must look horrified. Alice simply holds my hand. Two men step forward, and place a metal contraption the size of a small birdcage over Anne's head, with a spiked rod that goes into her mouth. She gags and coughs as they put it in, not particularly gently, and then I see a trickle of blood running down her chin. She can't move her mouth with this on. Probably not even her tongue.

All of this, for gossiping? Are you kidding me?

Anne wobbles over unsteadily to her bench, and sits back down with her family, hugging her children while simultaneously pushing them away from the cage. I'm sure it must be excruciating if they would pull on it. Some more prayers are said, a hymn is sung, and everyone agrees that this seems to be the funniest thing to happen in Cambridgeshire since the last time the Widow Johnson had one put on her. Of course, she had died in her home of asphyxiation without anyone able to help keep the weight off when she slept, so that was a shame, but in general, it's quite an amusing time.

I feel like the walls are caving in on me. I need to get out of here. Not just this church, but this island, this whole place. I try to breathe deeply, but I can't get away from what's happened. I am clearly stuck in hell.

CHAPTER EIGHT

A Plan

Fortunately for me the service ends just as I'm about to seriously lose it, and Alice helps escort me back out into the fresh air quickly. I take a moment to catch my breath, and then I gasp. "What the hell was that just now? And why does everyone think it's so funny?"

"It's the brank. The punishment for women gossiping or talking too much." She shrugs. "It's not nice. But it won't kill her. They'll leave it on for a week or so."

A week? A week walking around with that thing on your neck? I look back over as the family is coming out. Everyone is still looking at them, and a child throws an apple at Anne, who just tries to keep her head up. How can people think this is ok?

"It will provide some amusement and then remind her not to do something like that again," Alice says. "I'm not saying it's all fine. Just that it's not the worst thing that could have happened to her."

I don't want to know the worst thing, and fortunately Alice doesn't elaborate. The fresh air seems to be helping me feel a bit better, and Alice guides me over to a group of villagers who aren't laughing along with the others. The ones with the conscience, I think. Of course they're friends with Alice. She introduces me, and they look at me gratefully, happy to have someone else to distract them from the morning's show. They all show interest in knowing how a woman got from Somerset to London to Cambridge. I must be the most well-traveled woman around, they say. They ask me questions about what Glastonbury is like, about what London is like, hungry for information in this pre-internet disconnected world. I respond as best as I can.

"London is frantic, and busy. Messy. Garbage everywhere. The streets are so narrow you have to walk behind the cows half the time." Well, most of that is still true today. "Glastonbury is magical; a special place blessed by God," I say, which is also true.

They ask me what the roads were like from Glastonbury to London. They want to know about the pilgrims with whom I traveled, since no one had seen any. Oh, we separated back by Parker's Piece, I say, hoping that it exists, and if not, that no one realizes and they will all pretend to understand. They are all anxious for the latest news. They want to know what's happening with the King Henry's marital woes. They want to know what's happening to the men they've heard about. The king's ministers. They want court gossip. Someone wants to know if I've met their aunt, who bakes bread somewhere near St. Paul's.

After all that, I'm happy when Alice tells the others that I'm in need of rest after my journey, and we walk home. In her small cottage we silently make the lunch. Eggs from the hens, some carrots with herbs. Alice, I've noticed, has a largely vegetarian diet. I ask her about it. "I just love living things, and hate to eat them. Though I do when I need to obviously," she responds. Really, she's in the wrong century. She belongs in San Francisco in the 60s or something.

I spend the day helping her grind up her herbs, and then we make a vegetable stew over the fire for dinner. Throughout the day various people come in and out, asking for advice on health issues. A heavily pregnant woman, Susan, comes in. She hasn't felt her baby move in a little while, and is worried. Alice seems to be part midwife, part physician's assistant, part pharmacist, and part therapist. She gives the woman some peppermint tea with some honey, and some starchy grains, tells her to sit quietly for a few moments, and then after about 10 minutes the woman is happily feeling the baby again.

"Sometimes babies get tired and groggy and just need a bit of a wake up meal," she tells the woman, who leaves looking relieved and peaceful.

Another woman comes in who is having problems getting pregnant. Alice talks to her about her cycle, seeming to ask questions that are more advanced than I gave the 16th century credit for. She asks the woman about things like her cycle length, how often she and her husband lay down together, and all sorts of personal things. The woman answers with an honest and refreshing frankness. There isn't the squeamishness that I've noticed when I talk with other women about things like sex and pregnancy. After hearing the answers, Alice gives the woman some herbs.

"These should help," she explains, "If you take them in the middle of your cycle, made into a tea. Start around 5 days after you stop bleeding. Take them for 10 days." The woman walks out, happy.

Some men walk in as well. One man complaining about chest pains. Alice frowns. She gives him some herbs, tells him to rest, but after he leaves she looks despondent. "I've seen that before. I think his heart is just broken. Poor man. He lost his wife last year. Not much for him to live for now. They were true lovers." She makes the sign of the cross, so I do too.

During a lull she teaches me how to spin wool that she has carded, and I ask her if every day is as busy as this. "Oh, this is quiet," she says. "It's a Sunday," she explains. "People are at home resting." If this is quiet, I have no idea how she would ever get a moment to herself to think, but perhaps that's why people don't miss books or music. There really isn't that much time of solitude in which one needs to be entertained.

I turn my phone on to look at pictures of my family and friends again, and to listen to some music, but Alice tells me to do it in a corner where I won't be seen if someone comes in unannounced. Anyway, my break doesn't last long. My charge is down to 72%, and even though I have the solar powered charger, I haven't tested it yet, and have no idea how it will work.

Towards the end of the evening as the sun is setting, Matthew comes by. Alice looks pleased and offers him some stew with a chunk of bread. He asks me to sit next to him and he starts to talk.

"I told Brother Edward our story and he believed it, at least for now. You should be all right for the moment." Well, that's mildly reassuring.

"But, we really must get you protected by someone bigger and more important who has more influence than I am able to provide."

Uh oh. I don't like the sound of where this is going. I don't really want much more protection from more important people because the fact is, the fewer people who know I'm here, the better. The thing about being protected by big important people is that when they fall, which they invariably will during these turbulent times, you fall along with them.

I voice that concern to Matthew, but he stops me. "No, we need to figure out how to get you back, don't you see? Surely if you came here, you must be able to get back, and I want to help you. After I hear your take on the future of humanity," he smiles. "But bigger minds than mine need to work on it. We need for the important people at court to know about you."

"Oh no, no way, Matthew. I've watched The Tudors. I know what happens in that court. I am not interested in going anywhere near there. Anyway, who were you thinking could help?"

"I was once helped out of a tough spot by a distant cousin in London," he looks over at Alice as he says this. "You probably have never heard of him, but he works closely with the King, and his name is Thomas Cromwell."

Thomas Cromwell. The mastermind lawyer behind the king's divorce from Katherine of Aragon. But then he fell from grace and was killed. Hang on, what year are we in? And anyway, wasn't Cromwell a big Reformation proponent? How is our Brother Matthew hooked up with him?

"Matthew, I've heard of Cromwell, and that won't work."

"Why not?"

"Because he is going to have a fall, I'm afraid."

Matthew looks shocked.

"What, Master Cromwell? But the King depends on him for everything," he says.

"Yep. I believe his time is coming to an end very soon. You said we were in 1539, right? Has Henry married Anne of Cleves yet?"

"No but I hear that negotiations have been completed and they will wed early in the new year."

"Well, it won't be long then for Cromwell, I'm afraid."

Matthew looks down at his hands, despondent.

"And what of Anne of Cleves?"

"There's a rhyme we learned in school about Henry VIII and his six wives."

Matthew looks horrified. "Six wives he has?"

I nod and recite: "Divorced, beheaded, died. Divorced, beheaded, survived."

"Oh this is just awful. So Anne will survive, though divorced?" He's counting on his fingers, working out that she was the fourth wife.

"Yes, she will be given the title of the King's sister, which is a bit of a laugh. But poor Cromwell, who arranged the whole thing, will be the one who suffers the punishment."

Matthew looks down at the floor.

"These are such difficult times in which we live. May God have mercy on his soul. He was good to me once."

"The times are tough right now. The next twenty years or so are very tough for England. But some good comes of it, I guess. Queen Elizabeth is pretty awesome. Anyway, Matthew, how are you connected with a reformer like Cromwell?"

Giving me a sheepish grin Matthew lowered his eyes and said, "We are not all just innocents who follow the every whim of the Pope here in Cambridge, my Lady. Cambridge is known to have a strong reformist streak."

They just can't be very open about it yet, I think.

"So, since you seem to know so much about who is doing what in our Court, what would you recommend, Natasha?" he gets the conversation back on track. "We need someone who understands science. Who understands the way the world moves. We need someone with some knowledge of the new learning that is coming our way. We need to get the information you have so that we can use it to better ourselves."

"But don't you see Matthew, this is where it gets all strange. If you make changes based on things I tell you, surely that will have affected the future from which I come, because you will have changed things. So then the things I tell you become moot anyway. Because you would have already done them by the time my future happens. Isn't it enough to just give you a headache?"

Matthew sits quietly taking it all in.

"We need to do something though. Who do you know of who could help us figure this riddle out? I know you want to get home, and I want to get you home. You can't stay here. It just wouldn't work long term. I don't know where you could go, since you're a woman on your own. We could try to find you a husband, or put you in a convent, but I'm afraid that it would be incredibly difficult for you. And the husband or the nuns, for that matter," he laughs, and I smile at the truth of it. But it's a smile that comes with a shiver, thinking about how poor Anne with the birdcage on her head is doing tonight.

I sit and think about the various books I've read, the things I know about what is happening in the court and who the shining lights of scholarship are. The more I ponder, the more I realize it can't be someone high up in the Tudor court. It would be too dangerous. I know enough about that Court to know that I don't want to go nearer to it than I need to. I continue to sit in silence thinking, and then it comes to me.

"Richard Chancellor," I pull out the name, seemingly from nowhere. "Do you know him?"

"The name sounds vaguely familiar."

"He is a scholar. A Cambridge man. He leads a ship on a journey of exploration in the 1550's that was organized by Sebastian Cabot.So right about now he's probably studying and learning and becoming the explorer he will be later."

And I happen to know that he dies in one of his journeys, and so he won't be around to change things based on what I tell him.

Really, I picked a good time to come back to. If I'd have been stuck in Rome circa 200, or France circa 1789, I would have no idea what to do. And my dad said my medieval history degree would be useless. I laugh again at how lucky it is that I'm where I know at least a little bit about what's expected of me.

Matthew looks at me as I'm talking about Richard Chancellor and the journey of exploration that would take him around the Northern coast of Norway, into Russia's northern White Sea, and then down to Moscow.

"What amazing foreign things you know of," he says. He wants me to teach him everything I know. Even Alice stops cleaning up the wooden dishes long enough to listen as I tell them about the journeys to find new lands. They've heard news of the Spanish and Portuguese voyages to the Americas, but I tell them how England gets into the game with Jamestown and the early colonies, and it turns into a story about the Revolutionary War before I take a breath.

"I will do my best to contact Richard Chancellor," Matthew says once it's clear that I'm done. "Have you any idea where he studied? When he was here?"

Again I curse the fact that Google or Wikipedia won't work. But maybe it's a good thing. Surely poor Matthew would faint if he saw Wikipedia.

"I don't," I say. "All I know is that he was in London by the late 1540's getting ready for this journey he took in 1553. I know his wife had died leaving him with sons. He might already be married."

Matthew promises to search. "Is Sebastian Cabot back in England yet? Because he would be a route to finding Richard. I don't want Sebastian knowing about me, but if he knew that you were trying to hunt down Richard, he might be of help."

Again he nods, finishes his stew, and then asks to see my book again. He is fascinated by the paper. He wants to feel it, to touch it, to taste it, to practice writing with my pens. I really want to give him one, but I don't have that many, and anyway, I need to save something to give him as a thank you gift for his help. My cosmetics would be useless.

Finally, as the noises from other homes go quiet, and the sounds on the water turn to silence, Matthew quietly takes his leave with a quick but meaningful glance towards Alice, and then heads back to King's, his boat disappearing in the mists and cloudy sky.

CHAPTER NINE

The First Week

The following days were all similar to the first, only without the church service. Alice spent most of her time helping the villagers, and even some who came from Cambridge and the surrounding villages like Fen Ditton or Milton. I don't get much of a chance to think about my situation, nor do I wonder whether Matthew has located Richard Chancellor. I just sleep on my pallet with my furs, hide from the November rain, eat my porridge and vegetables, and help as I can. I prove inept at doing much of anything for Alice. I'm useless at housework. And she doesn't trust me to go on any errands for her thinking I would come off as clearly not from where I say I am (and she's right about that). So I mostly try to stay out of her way. The one job I can handle is spinning wool, and so most of my time is spent at the spinning wheel.

I wish there was a way I could pay her. I offer her my own money from 2015. She takes the bills and pound coins and stares at them. "A woman sovereign printed on such beautiful paper money. A queen," she repeats over and over. She asks me how medicine works in the 21st century. We spend much of our time talking, with me telling her about life where I come from. But I'm never sure how much I can say. One thing I quickly become conscious of is the difference in noise levels. In my London there is always a certain level of white noise of people talking on cell phones, the traffic, horns; even planes, music, announcements being made, sirens. There's rarely just complete quiet.

There isn't silence here either, but the noise is different. Conversations. Punting boats, and fishermen calling back and forth to each other. Children running around. Animals braying, having sex, or being slaughtered. There are so many different kinds of noises, and I'm never quite sure whether our conversations can be heard halfway across the village. Plus people seem to come into Alice's house without knocking; she is just so available to everyone.

I take a lot of comfort from her cats. She has three, all of whom are lovers. Paddy is the male who rules the roost, a big orange fellow who kneads into my skin while he's purring, which would be lovely if it didn't hurt so much. He has taken to sleeping with me at night, curling up in the furs by the fire with me and purring under my chin. I allow myself 20 minutes of phone time a day, and I show my little boy Paddy pictures of my parents, and my friends. Alice enjoys seeing pictures of Cambridge and London too, but she doesn't then purr into my shoulder afterwards.

The others are Genny and Tabby, both girls, one calico the other gray. They also are quite friendly, but given that they aren't "fixed" (there is no "fixing" here) they are a bit more moody. Falling asleep by the dying fire at the end of the day is my favorite time. I can close my eyes and think back to my walks around London, my favorite places on the Heath, in St. James's Park, in Soho. At one point I get excited thinking maybe I could figure out how to get to London now and see it, but then I remember that most of the London I am most familiar with doesn't exist. Soho is a hunting forest. Westminster Abbey would be there, though. Imagine the bliss at being able to go to an Evensong service there.

Though I suppose they wouldn't let common unmarried women into the service now.

But I can't really spend much time thinking about that. The 60 odd miles to London seem like an impossible distance. How could I get there? I could walk, but not on my own without a group to protect me. There is too much crime on the highways, which are really just paths. I remember a king, several hundred years before Henry, made a law that there should be an open space at least ten feet on either side of the paths so that criminals couldn't ambush travelers.

Surely I could find a group to travel with? It could be a sort of Canterbury Tales journey. But I would need to be introduced to them, I'd think? I resolve that if I'm stuck here for very long, I will ask Alice how it might be possible. She might even want to come along with me. Maybe we could go together, two girls going off to London to reinvent themselves and start new. But I suspect that there are things, or people, keeping her tied to Cambridgeshire.

As time passed that week, I found out more about Alice. Her parents died when she was very young in one of the many rounds of the plague that come back time and time again in the summer. “Happy in the morning, dead by dinner,” is how they often describe it. And that's how it was with her parents. Somehow she survived, and she went to live with her mother's sister, who was a kind woman but had many other children to care for. She couldn't spend time with Alice, who was more sensitive by nature than the other children, and help her nurture her gifts. Instead, they all saw Alice as odd, possibly possessed.

She ran away to the town of Cambridge, thinking perhaps she could earn some money as a seamstress to go towards a dowry to join a convent. Spending her life in quiet contemplation and closeness to God seemed like it would be a good decision. But she never was able to get to her community of prayerful sisters. She got pregnant, which meant that she would never ever be able to enter a convent as a clean and pure bride of Christ. Instead she would be expected to enter as a shamed woman, a sinner, who would be forced to leave the baby behind, and live her life not in quiet contemplation and sung prayer, but in repentance for her great sin and the great shame she had brought upon herself, the man in question, and the families involved.

The problem for her was that she never saw it as a sin. She wanted to keep the child. She thought she could see a way forward, even though the father was also tied to the Church. By that point she was already realizing that she had gifts of communication, of understanding how the earth works, and the gifts of healing that are provided through plants and herbs. Of being able to understand what was ailing people and help to make them better. So she decided that she would escape to one of the island villages in the fens, where she was unknown. She concocted a story about herself, and was still near enough to the father of her baby if he ever decided he wanted to be a part of its life, and she started scavenging for food and shelter.

Eventually her baby's father, who was an honorable (if fearful) man, gave her enough money to purchase a tiny plot of land on a swampy island 25 minutes by boat to the east of Cambridge, which had an already-built home. It had belonged to a widow whose husband died during the war against Scotland, and she had gone to live with one of her own children. Alice found the small settlement welcoming, and she found her neighbors friendly and supportive. She hunkered down and started to nest and prepare for her baby, a daughter, Rose, who arrived in May, snuggled and swaddled sleeping next to her.

They shared 5 months together, the two of them. Rose smiled and cooed and completely took ownership of Alice's heart. But then one crisp morning in October, Alice woke to find that Rose would not wake. Her breathing had stopped in the middle of the night, as so many small baby's breaths do stop, and for no reason. The grief crashed over her, wave after wave of it, consuming her, leaving her all alone in the world again, and with no hope of ever having a companion. She would never be able to find a husband after any potential man heard of her history. And the father would never make the same mistake again, she was sure of it.

He was immersed in the church and scholarship, and while he bitterly regretted the loss of baby Rose, he felt that it must be payment for his sin, which led him even deeper into the arms of the church. Alice was well and truly alone, though surrounded by people who seemed to understand her pain and were protective of her. Now ten long autumns later, she found some solace in her work of healing others, she had goddaughters and godsons around the county, but she would always have the pain of waking up to her cold lifeless tiny daughter; having to bury her, having to endure the stares of strangers who didn't know her, but still felt as if they were familiar enough with her to be able to make conclusions and judgements about her.

And, I thought, she still had to see Matthew, who I'd worked out early on must be the father. She still has something going on with him, and until she can really leave him behind, she'll never be able to start something fresh. That realization struck me as I considered my own life, and my own inability to leave people behind and start fresh. Her story hit home because I too had carried a small baby in my belly, had thought I could nurture it and love it even though I would have been a single parent, and lost it. I thought about how so much of my own recent descent into sloth and vice has come from the fact that I was still completely hung up on someone that I fell in love with when I was 29, and who rejected me then, though he left me pregnant. That was over five years ago for me, and the more time went by, the more the realization would set in that I really wasn't going to ever grow old with him, and the guilt that I had lost his baby. Then I would seek out another bar, another warm body, some kind of substance to keep me from remembering how much pain I was in.

As much as I wouldn't want to diminish anyone's pain, least of all my own, I knew that the pain of not being loved by a romantic interest was nothing compared to the loss of a child. Even my own loss had only happened a few weeks in. It still hurt, and was still driving my life in many ways, but it couldn't compare to the loss of a living smiling baby with whom one has fallen in love. Grief is grief, and I can't compare my loss to hers, but it was startling to think that here Alice was, going about life and thriving, while I reacted with the cliched alcohol and sex. I should look to Alice as an example of what I could do with my own life, how I could be productive even in the face of heartache.

These were the things I would think about and ponder the more I got to know Alice. And as Paddy would crawl under the blankets with me and curl up next to my chest, I would wrap my arm around him, close my eyes, and daydream about the walks I had taken through the London I knew, the Cambridge I knew, and even drives along the 210 freeway in Los Angeles. I supposed I would never see the traffic on the 210 into Pasadena at rush hour again. It made me laugh, that I missed the jammed 605 interchange.

I thought about trying to describe rush hour traffic to Alice, and I knew that anything I could say wouldn't come close to describing the frustration of sitting in eight lanes of stop and go traffic for an hour, and it would also would make us all sound idiotic. We spend

3 hours a day in a little pod trapped on a freeway so we can get to jobs we don't like so we can get money to buy gadgets like new iPhones so we can play Angry Birds in HD and distract ourselves from the misery and drudgery that our lives have become. Thinking about it now, it sounds ridiculous. No wonder people have a midlife crisis. Just as I looked at Alice as if she was slightly backwards for eating raw onions right out of the ground, I'm sure she would react to me as if I was one of the most backwards people on the planet if I explained to her the extent to which modern people will go to not have to be present to our own lives.

CHAPTER TEN

Market Day

I got a break with some excitement on Thursday of that week as Alice said we could go into Cambridge for market day to get some cloth and other supplies to make me look like I actually belonged in the 16th century.

Thursday morning we got up earlier than normal, which is saying something. The rooster was still asleep. It was dark and quiet, and almost eerie as everything on the island was silent. We ate our normal breakfast of cheese, an onion (which is much sweeter than onions I eat on sandwiches) and some mead. Then Alice gathered up some clay bowls she made that she was taking to barter. I felt another surge of shame, costing her even more money that I know she doesn't have, but there was nothing I could really do about it, and anyway, I suspected that Matthew would be giving something back to her.

The bowls were created from the silty swampy mud in the bottom of the fens, the land which, after the fens were drained, became so fertile. She would shape them, then leave them out to dry, and then make a kiln in her fireplace. Some were deep, and others were more shallow, but they were all made with love and care, and her fingers showed the stains if you looked closely. I watched her wrap them in wool and carry them awkwardly to the boat where one of the neighbors, John, was meeting us to take us to town. I really needed to build her a crate of some sort. That was a way I could be useful. I assume there must be hammers and nails around somewhere, though I was guessing that finding ready-cut 2x4's would be harder than simply going to Home Depot.

We made the journey by boat back the way I came on Saturday night with Matthew, but this time in the growing daylight I could see everything, which made it that much more interesting. As the fens came alive with birds and fish all around us, the fog lifted, and the sun shimmered on the water. In the distance I could see the Chapel of King's College, a beacon of light and hope just as it was meant to be. But everything else was different. There was no railway. No train station. No paved roads with busses. No Marks and Spencer. No Cafe Nero.

The ride took just under half an hour. We docked by a part of the river near where Jesus Green is now. I got off the boat and wandered around among the others who were bringing wares to market, or coming to make purchases. I looked for the Pizza Express which is in a row of new condos, but of course it wasn't there. None of it was there. Just dilapidated wooden shacks. We left John after agreeing to meet with him just after noon, and then walked over to King's Parade. Now this I knew.

The street actually didn't look that much different than now, if you just looked from knee level up. Below, it was awful. We trudged along through dung and excrement of all the animals who were being led to the market. There was no way for the streets to drain, and they weren't cleaned, so there was just grime and crud all over everything. The buildings appeared to have had feeble attempts made to keep them clean, but it didn't really work. And the smell! The smell was atrocious. Excrement mixed with the body odor of an entire town where people never bathed. Plus, added to that the stale swampy air. Even in November the bugs were still out in the street, swarming around animals and anyone who got near them.

But the buildings, and the stories in those buildings! Most of the buildings have changed. Trinity was under construction. How exciting it was to stand outside and see that red brick rising up, knowing what it would become later, the statue of Henry VIII that would look over the street, showing off his huge codpiece. It took all my energy not to take a picture with my cell phone. That would have been nearly impossible to explain. I wondered whether I would ever have time alone in the city, if it would be empty enough so that I could take a few pictures surreptitiously.

As we got closer to King's and the market, I asked Alice if we could wander through the alleyway back to the river, just so I could see it. She was nervous since the land belonged to the colleges and we weren't meant to be near it, but I must have given her puppy dog eyes because she relented in the end. So we walked through the little maze of buildings on the uneven stone roads, and wound up behind the colleges, where the arched bridges cross the river, and the scene actually looked nostalgic and familiar to me. For a moment I could focus only on the back of King's and pretend I had gone punting and I would be going back for a nice warm dinner at a pub somewhere where there were loud football fans.

But no, in the end a robed scholar was crossing the lawn and Alice freaked out, and dragged me back towards the open market. It was odd for me to be there. There's still a market in the square today. Only now the vendors sell incense. And natural soap. And honey, and all manner of random products like that mixed with tourist souvenirs. But this market was different. It was full of color and noise, the sound of people bartering and catching up with neighbors and friends they only saw on Market days. There were goats. Live goats. And cows, and other animals. Lots of chickens.

Eggs. People selling wool. People selling finished cloth, though not much because most couldn't afford it. There were some people selling ready made pasties, which looked absolutely delicious - I hadn't had any ready made food since I'd been with Alice - but they were also expensive, and I was already costing her too much, so I just stared longingly at them.

We headed for the woman she knew who made fabric from some of the wool that Alice would spin for her. The woman, Jane, looked at me curiously and Alice explained my story. I was Margaret, and I had come from London with pilgrims on their way to Ely. I really needed to remember that properly. I didn't have anything, needing to flee my home, and not having much support. And so she was buying me cloth to make some clothing. Jane was a kind soul and gave us some of her ugliest and oldest unfinished cloth in exchange for three pieces of pottery, which I was certain she would turn back around and sell for much more than she had paid. But that wasn't my fight. I gratefully took the bundle of cloth, and then followed Alice to a cobbler who could sell her some leather to make me shoes. He heard the same story, took pity on us since he also knew Alice, and one bowl bought us a nice strip of very raw leather that I would wrap around my feet with leather straps he included. They would help keep the cold out of my toes, at least. And for that I was grateful again. Winter was coming soon. I could stuff some wool around my feet, and then cover them with leather, and I would be as good as new. It wouldn't be quite like wearing my cozy Uggs, but it would be better than going barefoot. At night I slept in my regular warm boots because no one would be coming in to catch me in them, but for day I really needed something that would fit in. And so, boots of a sort would be crafted.

Alice took stock of the bowls that were left, and decided that she would treat us to some fresh fruits that came all the way from Spain. Oranges and other exotic fruits that had traveled by boat up the Atlantic, avoiding pirates along the French coast, across the English channel, and were unpacked at Dover and brought by wagon the 120 miles or so up here. The whole journey from Spain would have taken less than two weeks. Thank goodness oranges have a long shelf life.

She also bought some unprocessed grain, and then we were going to head back, with our packages and bundles under our arms and hugged tightly to our chest where my phone rubbed against my skin. I still always kept my phone and some modern money and a pen and notebook in my bra - if I ever got separated from Alice and something bad happened, I was going to need to prove myself. And it was nice having those comforting things with me.

Before we headed back to the boat to meet John, who would take us back to our village island, I wanted to explore just a tiny bit more. "I know this town," I said to Alice. "I want to see it like it was before." I knew I'd possibly never get to London, but there was no reason why I shouldn't be able to play tourist in Cambridge while I was here. We wandered past King's down to Queen's, which had been started by Margaret of Anjou and Elizabeth Woodville, the two warring queens. The houses of Lancaster and York, uniting in scholarship and the raising up of young minds. It was a stunning crisp day, the kind of day you get right as winter sets in, as a reminder of what you'll be missing, and the hope of what will come if you survive the winter. And in the 16th century, survival of the winter was a real thing that you had to worry about.

I enjoyed walking along the cobblestones, but Alice was nervous. As much as she was comfortable in town among her friends and acquaintances, she was antsy and jittery around the colleges.

"Why are you so uncomfortable here?" I asked.

"They don't like me here. They think I'm evil. Some of them think I shouldn't be allowed to be where I am. I think they feel threatened by me. Because I took one of their own and made him sin," she smiled sadly. "As long as I stay in my place they are ok and don't bother me too much. But if I start to stray into their territory again, they don't like it. They've threaten to hurt me."

Again I wonder at the wisdom of her staying around here. What, I wonder, does she think will come of this? Is Matthew suddenly going to leave his life of study and join her in her village? Are the educated professors and scholars suddenly going to accept her as one of their own? I feel like she's holding on to a pipe dream. But then, I did that too. For a long time. I still do it, I know. So I understand.

We walk back to the boat quietly. The sun will be setting soon - it is November after all and the days are short. I may have been asking for too much in hoping the rain and dark would stay away. I remember the cozy cottage and am looking forward to getting back there to our fireplace and our friendly neighbors. Suddenly I see Cambridge through Alice's eyes - full of sinister men who judge her as a jezebel and want to punish her for her infraction. And on her behalf, also being a woman who has had what they would term "loose morals" I want to go. The adventure of being in Cambridge today had been amazing, but I was ready to get back to the safety and comfort of the cottage.

We meandered back through the tiny dirty streets to where the watermen were waiting to take market visitors back, and we found John, who hadn't been waiting too long, and was also laden down with purchases and trades. We packed everything in the boat, which was already wet from the mist that was rolling in. I thought about my English geography, and remembered the mists rolling in off the coast when I'd spent a night in Harwich on a ferry to Holland, which couldn't go because even with all their sophisticated GPS and radar, it still wasn't safe in the fog. So we sat there, rolling and tossing with the tide. I'd walked around the boat, trying to find the bars and drink away my sea sickness.

That was right at the beginning of my downward decline, just over five years ago. I had come to terms with the fact that I was probably going to turn 30 and still be unmarried. And I decided that it would be a good idea to start to party as if I would be 29 forever. Looking back on it now from the distance of 500 years (and nearly a week of being sober, doing manual labor, and attending almost-daily prayer services with enforced meditations) I can see how abusive I was to myself. But I didn't see it at the time. All I saw at the time was the relentless pursuit of pleasure and distancing myself from the pain.

We traveled on the Cam around Jesus Green, and then eventually veered off towards the little island I was now beginning to think of as home. The grass was still green, even in November. In return for the beautiful frost-free grass, we still had the bugs, I guess. But it was chilly enough that they largely left us alone, and I sat enjoying the quiet, watching the scenery. I'd never traveled through this part of the country before, even by train, and certainly not by boat, and I again fell in love with England. I had come here on holiday when I was 24, and fallen in love with the scenery, with the green rolling hills, with the seaside, with the history. At every turn on every street you ran into history. Oh yes, here's another Norman castle built by William after the Conquest. Here are the remains of a Viking invasion. Oh yes, and here, in the bottom of an art gallery, while you're hanging out looking at art, you can just walk down three flights of stairs and be in an original Roman arena. No biggie. Just another day of walking around in England.

I resolved to come back and make my life in this world that was so connected to its past, which was such a change from where I lived in Los Angeles, where everything stretched out for infinity into the desert. Don't like your house? Tear it down and build a new one. There's so much room. An abundance of supplies. Hell, Congress even degreed that we should have all the water we can ever want thanks to the Aqueduct. Remember that the Spanish were here first? And before them, the Native Americans? That there were entire thriving cultures here before we made it a wonderland of make believe? Nah. Let's put giant letters up on the hillside. And build earthquake proof buildings. Let's build a giant museum funded by oil money that is destroying the environment up on a hillside that is bisected by a freeway, and put some of the world's most precious art in it and make it nearly impossible for anyone who doesn't have a car to enjoy it.

In London, the National Gallery is in the middle of Trafalgar Square. Anyone can walk in during their lunch break and stare at a Da Vinci Virgin on the Rocks for half an hour, stop at Pret a Manger and grab a sandwich, catch the end of a free concert in St. Martin's in the Fields (home of the, "it's Tuesday, it must be Vivaldi to appeal to the tourists" orchestra) and be back in the office for the afternoon. It's how I spent my first years in London. Working in the heart of publishing in Bedford Square in Bloomsbury, spending my time wandering around the museums, discovering hidden places. The house that Benjamin Franklin lived in during his stay in London. The home of William Blake, which is now a waxing salon.

The ancient City churches built by Christopher Wren after the Great Fire which dominated London's skyline before the skyscrapers came along, and have amazing lunchtime concerts that are begging for audiences. Of course, that was the scene of the beginning of my Downward Spiral, but we'll forget about that for the purpose of this conversation. Leandenhall Market. The British Museum. I would carry my A-Z with me (it was before the days of Google Maps) and go out on missions of discovery every lunch hour, long walks along the river, the South Bank, Borough Market and Southwark Cathedral across from the City of London, where the prostitutes used to congregate under the protection of the Bishop of Winchester, who happily benefited from the taxes on their revenue.

This was how I started out my time in London. And because I was a hard worker, I got jobs. I had companies sponsor me and get me a work visas. I proved my worth, and I brought in money. Eventually I went from being an editorial assistant with a most-likely-illegal bedsit in a council flat in Highgate to a larger garden flat in Hampstead when I was promoted to Junior Editor. Then eventually buying my own home in Muswell Hill complete with a garden flat of its own that I could rent out to help pay the mortgage, and which I stopped renting out when I became the youngest ever Editor-in-Chief at Court Magician. My star was rising, and it seemed as if everything was going wonderfully for me. And that's when it all started falling apart.

But here I was now, on this slow moving boat punting through the fens, watching the world go past with my new good friend and a warm cottage with cats to go back to. No internet. No DVR'd episodes of Made in Chelsea. No warm bath. But it seemed to be ok. I was still hoping that I would be able to get back. After all, if I was able to get here in the first place, surely I would be able to get back. If I stopped to think about it too much my head would explode. Was I aging? Say I was here for a decade. Would I return back to 2015 being 45? Or 35? And was time passing there? Did I miss my meeting with Howard? I kind of wished I'd watched Back to the Future more closely. Eventually I stopped thinking and just enjoyed the feeling of the boat moving along, and listening to Alice and John chit-chat.

When we got home, after checking on all the animals and making some pottage in the pot on the fire, Alice set to work making me my dress, and I began fashioning my shoes from the leather and wool. They weren't pretty, but they would work, and by the time I went to bed that night I was the proud owner of a stylish dress, and footwear. Definitely a successful trip to Market.

CHAPTER ELEVEN

Richard Chancellor

Time passed monotonously. The thing that really struck me about life in the mid-16th century is how alike every day was, completely indiscernible from the day before. Every day we woke up at the same time with the roosters. Literally. We built a fire right away which would be kept going throughout the day. Every day we saw most of the same people. We ate some porridge. We ate some root vegetables. We salted and packed some freshly slaughtered meat that we prayed would last us through the winter. We preserved some fruits and vegetables from the autumn harvest. We went to evening prayer at the little wooden church with the fat abbots and the stinking incense. We talked to people. We ate more food. We communed with animals. Alice tried to heal people. Many times she was successful. Then we snuggled down under our furs, each with a cat or two, and fell asleep. It was the same thing over and over. Very little variation. No travel. The excitement was if someone had died. Sometimes there were birthdays celebrated. Or Saint's Feast Days. But I guessed that for me that would only serve to heighten the drudgery of the rest of the time.

I suppose the same sorts of things could be said about our time. How we go to the same jobs every day, and sit in the same offices or the same cubicles. And how we talk to mostly the same people. And our jobs really didn't change that much. And we have several weeks of holiday a year, but really, how many of us do anything exciting with it? Mostly we'd continue to check emails on our phone, and if we went somewhere exotic we would spend the entire time worrying about what we were missing back in the office, the one that we didn't even like being in the first place. I'm not sure which group is ultimately better off, but I was starting to see the merits of Alice's way.

I managed to make it through another two weeks without giving myself away, or causing Alice too much grief. I spent any down time looking at the pictures on my phone. I had tested the solar powered charger on a sunny day, and it worked well, so I was confident enough that I even listened to some of my music from time to time, and took some photos of Alice, which caused her no end of excitement when she saw what she really looked like. She'd never actually seen herself before except in reflections on the water. There were no mirrors, and glass was only in the wealthiest of homes. She and I spent one entire evening laying in bed taking selfies of each other with the cats, giggling like schoolgirls.

In the middle of the third week Matthew came again. Alice lit up when she saw him approaching in his robes, and she pinched her cheeks discreetly to get the color flowing, probably hoping I wouldn't notice. But I did notice. And I noticed the way his hand stayed on hers a little too long when he greeted her. He sat down and started talking right away, not even waiting for the customary offer of mead or gruel.

"I have discovered Richard Chancellor, and you're right, he's in Cambridge. He is coming to my room tomorrow."

"Oh Matthew!" I wanted to hug him.

My heart leapt. I had read about this man, and though I knew his life would be cut short, I also knew that he was a brilliant mathematician, and a scholar who was versed in modern ways of thinking. If anyone could understand my predicament and help me, he could. I was sure of it. I didn't have access to Copernicus or Da Vinci, but I felt sure that Richard Chancellor would do in a pinch.

"So you will come? To my rooms? At King's off the Chapel? Do you remember how to get there? Alice can spare you?" He glanced up at her, and she was smiling as well, and nodding. We had grown close enough in the past couple of weeks that my joy was now her joy.

"Of course I will be there, and of course I know how to get there." I was so impatient. I literally could not wait for tomorrow. I wanted Chancellor to be here now. Right this instant.

Matthew didn't stay for any food, but immediately went back to King's. I was so grateful that he had taken the time to make this connection and help me. I'm sure he had his own motives; he wanted to know what sort of magical messages I brought from God, which I wasn't sure I could help with. But for now, I was just overflowing with gratitude.

That night I could barely sleep. I was wide awake in bed, snuggling with Paddy in the furs, thinking about the things I wanted to discuss with Richard Chancellor. I would have to tell him a bit about what was coming for him, and I was going to have to tell him the little bit I knew about Einstein and the theory of relativity, and the specials I'd seen on time travel, and whether it could be true that all times were happening at once, and I just got thrown into a different dimension or something.

The things that make my head spin and give me a headache. No biggie. I considered what I had learned in Physics in high school. I tried to remember everything I could about algebra and math. With Paddy purring in my ear, I got in a meditative state and did my best to remember Newton and the scientific discoveries that I knew would be coming in the next hundred years, that a man like

Chancellor could use now to further his career, and perhaps understand enough to be able to see the same puzzle pieces that I was looking at, and put them together in a way that I couldn't.

Eventually I fell asleep thinking about force equalling mass times acceleration, gravity, the planets spinning, the rotation of the earth, the exploration of the poles, true north, and other scientific advances that I was going to need to catch Chancellor up on if he was going to be able to help me. I dreamt again about being in London in my time, only I was in a lecture hall in the Science Museum in Kensington learning about time travel from Robbie Williams.

I woke up the next morning feeling even more tired than I was before I went to sleep, but I was also so excited at the meeting with Richard Chancellor. I was antsy and irritable, and pushed Paddy away when he tried to snuggle up. When Alice gave me a chunk of bread with some chicken stock for breakfast I could barely eat any of it.

Eventually the waterman, Joseph, came from King's to take me back to Matthew's. I asked Alice if she was coming - the idea of making the half an hour journey on my own with a stranger wasn't particularly appealing to me. She didn't feel comfortable going there, of course, and I wondered why I even asked as I stepped into the small boat. She waved to me from the marshy rushes on the shore. As we pulled out I clutched my phone, which I had wrapped in one of the pieces of the leather she bought to make my shoes, and tucked it into the hemp bag that I was carrying. Also inside the bag were my proof that I come from a time in the future - the book, some modern money, and my other gadgets.

Joseph tried to make conversation with me, but I intimated that I didn't understand him very well, and so he stopped after a few moments, which made me happy. Even in my real life, I'm not a big fan of chatting with taxi drivers.

As King's came into view I relaxed and tried to make myself as warm as possible in my furs. I was so close to getting my journey back home started again, and while I knew I wasn't going to be able to do it overnight, at least I could start to feel like I was working towards something, and taking steps forward. Not just stagnant and resigned to living in 1539.

Matthew was pacing on the bank of the river waiting for me, and when he saw me he covered me in a cloak, pulled the hood over my head, bustling me into the Chapel, where the other brothers and scholars barely gave me any notice with my head down. I looked just like one of them in my robe. It felt so odd being back here again, in the daylight without the spooky feeling of the spirits of Halloween like the first time I was here with him.

When we entered Matthew's room Richard Chancellor was already there. A small man (though everyone in the 16th century seems to be small) with shoulder length brown hair, he was about twenty and bright eyed, looking eagerly my way as he stood up and smiled. I noticed that his smile is easy, and he looked incredibly bright. I got a very good feeling from him.

"This is the woman? From the future?" He came over and clutched my hand. I looked at Matthew, disappointed that he's been telling people about me already. I thought it was my secret to tell. It seemed like Richard could tell what I was thinking because the next thing that came out of his mouth is, "I assure you, Madam, I have told no one, and the only reason Matthew told me was to get me to meet you - I was suspicious of him and did not want to answer his call. But I am so glad that I did come."

I tried to get some dignity together. After all, I knew way more about science before I was in high school than he knows now. And

I know how the globe looks. I needed his help, but only so that he can help me put together this puzzle, while I am the one providing the pieces.

"Mr. Chancellor, since you already know my story, would you like to see proof?"

He gasps as I take out the book and notebook and gel pens. These Pilot gel pens sure are a hit. I wish I could give one to everyone I meet, but then I wouldn't have any left for myself, and if I'm going to be here for a while, I'm going to need them. I don't think I could figure out how to write with a quill this late in life. Old dog, new tricks.

Finally I take out my gadgets, the kit I pull out to prove to the world here that I am from the time I say I am. My ipad and phone, and my kindle, with the small amount of charge that's left. I take a picture of them with the ipad, and then show it to them on the screen, which makes Richard cross himself. I find a video of myself in modern London that I show them, walking with a friend through Hyde Park on a particularly glorious summer day. There are cars in the pictures, and people talking on cell phones. Modern clothing. Modern buildings. They are dutifully amazed.

Chancellor sits down in a chair, and looks as if he's going to make himself comfortable. He asks me many questions about scientific discoveries. I draw a picture of the world for him, and show him where I'm from in Los Angeles. I draw England and Scotland, Ireland, Iceland, Greenland. He begins to believe my map is genuine when I show him places that have only recently been discovered, and that only those who are in the circle of discoverers (and those who follow them) would know.

I give him the brief overview of Newtonian physics, of the laws of motion as I can remember them. He gasps when I tell him that the world goes around the sun, and that there are millions and billions of suns, each with orbiting earths going around them in the giant universe. I tell him about the Hubble Telescope, about the moon landing, about the planets, about the Kuiper belt, the milky way, and everything I can remember from planetarium trips. I talk to him about mathematics, about calculus and how it solves the equations of motion. I tell him about radar and how ships will be sailed in the future.

And then I tell him about Einstein, and how he shook up the laws of Physics. About the theory of relativity. I talk about the very fast speeds at which humans can move in my time, and how distance and time seem relative. I give him equations from Einstein - velocity = distance divided by time for example. I explain the little bit I know about how that could affect time travel. He makes a good show of taking it all in, nodding sometimes, looking shocked at others. I wonder whether maybe, in my eagerness to find someone who can help me, I am throwing too much at him. His head must be aching. But when I'm done with my lecture, which seems like hours, he looks at me in wonderment.

Matthew has been trying to take notes, scratching away on parchment with his quill, but gave up and now just stares at me, then says to Richard, "I told you she had secrets to share with us." Richard laughs, and then looks at me. "Since you know all of this, my lady, why do you need my help?"

"Look, Richard. Can I call you Richard? In the 21st century we aren't nearly as formal as you are here. So I'm going to call you Richard. I don't know how I got here. I have no idea. I have this knowledge and I need someone to help me use it. I think you could take the parts that I've given you, and help me construct a theory, or something to help me get back home. In return, I'm giving you knowledge that is going to help your career beyond what you can dream. I happen to know for a fact that you will go on to pilot major voyages of exploration, and discover new lands, and I think it's because of the knowledge I'm giving you right now. So see, we're meant to be having this discussion.

Richard looks down at the notes Matthew hands him, and sighs. "I do not know if I can rise to what is asked of me. It's such a unique situation."

"Look you guys," I say, dipping back into modern parlance. "I do not belong here. I do not belong in a place where you don't take baths. Seriously, Cambridge smells like shit, and that's not a euphemism. You all smell. You don't notice it because you all smell the same, but seriously, this century stinks. I need to be in a place with running water, hot and cold, and good coffee. And chocolate. And cheap books. And warm mattresses with wonderful duvets. And washing machines. And McDonald's. And trains. And my family. And my friends. As much as I love the history here, I do not belong in 16th century England. Anyway, I just gave you enough information to make you the most famous mariner in history if you use it right. You owe me now."

They both stare at me with open mouths after my monologue, and I notice Matthew surreptitiously sniffing his robe. Richard looks as if he has seen the light, so to speak. "I will do whatever I can to help, madam," Richard says. "It appears to be a challenge that I would enjoy. And you're right that you say it could help my career. I long to captain a voyage," he says dreamily.

CHAPTER TWELVE

Philosophizing with Matthew

The conversation goes on for a long time. Richard asks me for every detail of what I remember from my journey, if you can call it that. We walk out to the Chapel and Matthew points out exactly where he found me, and I show them where I was sitting. We talk about how the room turned black and how I lost consciousness. Richard looks like he's writing everything down in his head, and does a lot of nodding.

Eventually Richard begs off. His wife is pregnant, he says, and she will want him home soon. We agree to meet again in a week's time. After he goes, Matthew wants to walk and talk theology. It's still light, and warmer than it has been, so we go outside to the green where we can get some fresh air.

We sit on the grass in the main courtyard, and I pull out my solar powered charger to add some juice to my phone. Wearing my robe and sitting with Matthew, I can more easily blend in, and hide the charger, and people will take less notice to the gadget between us. I position Matthew across from me so that the small solar receptors are slightly hidden from passers by, but still are getting enough to give me a bit more life in my battery.

Matthew has picked up on the same theological argument that caused Copernicus to die. If the earth orbits the sun, and not the other way round, then we are not the center of the universe the way the Bible promises. How are we able to make sense of that in the modern days?

I respond as best as I can with the limited theological knowledge I have. It's never been an issue for most Christians I know, I tell him, including myself. I don't really want to get into Evolution with him, but I do talk about the Big Bang, and about all of the potential energy of the entire universe fitting into a tiny little dot smaller than his pinky nail, and from that came everything we are now. That little dot of energy, I tell him, that is God. God has created us as the center of everything but it's so much bigger than we know. Infinity is so mind boggling. The relative position of the planets has very little to do with the relationship we have with Divinity, I tell him.

We sit there, with my phone charging, and I talk to him about history. About the religious struggles in Europe for the next hundred and fifty years. About the Huguenots in France, and the St. Bartholomew's Day Massacre when thousands of Protestants were killed throughout Paris as thugs joyfully murdered them in the name of their God. About the colonization of America and the millions of Native Americans who died for empire. About slavery and how it was justified in the Bible, but eventually we came to realize as a society that it was wrong. And I told him about the Holocaust, and the systematic extermination of an entire race.

We talked about the idea of the Other, and how easy it is to blame people who aren't like you for your problems. And then I even start to touch on gay marriage and women priests, which I can tell makes him very uncomfortable, but I give him credit for listening to me and not just turning away. I talk about the idea that we all worship the same God, but He manifests Himself in many different ways to people in forms that they can understand based on their cultures and histories. It's really enjoyable, talking about theology and science like this with someone whose mind is so clearly being blown.

"You could say in closing, I suppose, that history seems to be on a long march towards giving people more rights, towards being more accepting of each other, towards understanding that there are shades of gray and interpretations of Scripture can change over the course of history based on revelations and being moved by the Holy Spirit."

He looks thoughtful. "But surely sin must be punished, otherwise how would society keep any order. And surely God's law can only have one meaning? You can't have multiple interpretations about the Truth, can you?"

I point out the changes in his own church that are going on right now. "Don't you see, Matthew. Both sides think they're right. And both sides are willing to die, and to kill, for being right. Both sides think there's only one way, and they are the ones who have the way. Even smaller reforms, which I know many Catholics are willing to make, are still changing the way the church is run, and if you do that over 500 years, even without the schisms and the atrocities of the Holocaust, slavery, and everything like that, you're still going to wind up with a more liberal church. The church today certainly looks a bit different than it did in the year 1000, right? I mean, that was before Thomas Aquinas, and the mystics, and the Great Schism when there were two Popes, right? I mean, how do you justify that? Which one was correct? They both thought they were. Anyway, sometimes Matthew, you move slowly towards reform, and other times terrible things make people sit down and really do some thinking and looking inwards to see if they are on the right track, and if changes need to be made."

He is still looking at me thoughtfully. "Then have all wars ended by your time?" I sigh.

"I wish, Matthew. I wish. Humans are still humans, and we haven't gotten there yet. Men may marry men, but there are still crazy fundamentalists who spoil it all for the rest of us, who are just trying to get through life doing the best we can."

He's quiet for a while, thoughtful.

"Do you go to church regularly in your time?" he asked, seemingly out of nowhere.

I think about it. I used to go to church for the Evensong services, back in those happy days when I first moved to London. Before I became a hot mess. Maybe if I'd kept going, things might not have turned out as miserably as they had. Maybe if I'd have stayed focused on what was important to me - the music, the history. But it was just so hard.

So here's where it all comes out. There was my great love. Paul. Paul Cooper. Just saying his name makes my breath quicken with lust, nervousness, and embarrassment. He was an organist at Saint Bride's church, one of Christopher Wren's architectural creations after the Great Fire of London. I used to go to evening prayer service after work. It was a ritual of mine, to check out the various sung prayer services at all the ancient churches in London.

I noticed him right away, and what I noticed was his back because that was all I could see. What an odd thing to be the first impression of someone, but it was so strong, and I could see the muscles moving as his fingers ran over the keys and his legs moved to reach the pedals. Playing the organ is an incredibly physical experience, and I'd never noticed it before watching him.

I hung around the church afterwards, pretending to look at my A-Z and figure out where I was headed next, but watching the choir leave and trying to make sure I didn't miss him. And I didn't. He walked out from a back room, down the center aisle, pausing in the back to bow to the altar, and then turned and saw me. I made eye contact, and then looked away, feeling a nervous flutter in my chest.

He walked over and sat down next to me.

"Are you lost?" he pointed to my A-Z sitting on my lap.

I smiled. No, I'm found, I thought. Very very found.

"Just trying to figure out my next move," I responded, feeling cryptic but honest.

"I noticed you watching me during the service," he said simply.

"Yes. Well, I never really paid much attention to the organ before. I never realized how much goes into it, I guess."

"There's a really good pub down the road that does amazing roast dinners. Would you..."

"Yes," I blurted out before he could even finish asking.

And that was it. It was fate, I thought. I became consumed by him, losing myself in him and discovering parts of myself that I never dreamed existed. He was my air and my life and my love. The problem was that he didn't feel the same way about me.

After that first date, he didn't call right away. I was floating on cloud nine, watching my phone for a text or call, daydreaming at the office (something I never did) and when an email finally came in it was noncommittal. Here I'd thought we had the most perfect first date ever, but for him this was just another thing to do after service. I asked around, various musical friends, and found out that he was known as a guy who liked to create girl drama. His signature move was just what he had done with me. Find a chick who was impressionable, and impress her.

But I felt sure that I could help him mend his womanizing ways. I was positive that if he could just get to know me properly, he would see in me what I saw in him; a spiritual love that was music and poetry and angels singing. I built him up in my head so that he became this goal I had to achieve. I just couldn't fathom the idea that I could be so passionate about someone who couldn't see how perfect we were together.

And so I kept calling. I was a borderline stalker. Finally he agreed to meet up with me for a second date, and we had a Mexican dinner that was the definition of awkward. Avoiding eye contact, making small talk, with me trying desperately to be the woman that I thought he would want. I'm not sure now how I could have become so lost in someone.

We both got drunk to avoid the stilted conversation, which is what many British people do when they are in an uncomfortable situation. And somehow, after a few too many glasses of pinot grigio, we were in a cab with him ripping my clothes off, headed back to my place.

It wasn't lovemaking. It wasn't even really all that passionate. I could tell it was pity sex. I knew right away by how quickly he left that there was nothing remotely romantic about it. It was a job he felt he needed to do, and leave as quickly as possible after. Like, ok, you wanted to see the cosmic lovemaking we could create, here's some sloppy sex to show you we really aren't that good together.

I curled up into a ball after he left and cried because I felt so alone. I could tell right away what had happened, and I knew that it wasn't the connection that I had felt. I was disappointed and lonely, I was homesick and tired, and I was hurt.

Work beckoned, and I lost myself in a new project for several weeks, trying not to think about him, and pushing him from my mind when he did come up. He was always there waiting to come back in, though. How could someone you knew for such a short time, who clearly didn't like you the way you adored them, make such an impact on you?

And then I realized I was late.

I'd always had sporadic periods, so I didn't think much about it right away. I just had this sudden fleeting feeling that my period should have come already, and that it was weird that it hadn't. I chalked it up to being busy and stressed at work, nurturing a broken heart, and a cold I had fought.

It still didn't come. I thought back to my previous cycles, and tried to remember the last time I had my period, and I couldn't. It must have been about ten weeks or so. Right around the time I had met Paul, I thought. Which would have put me about two weeks into my cycle when we had the sloppy drunk pity sex.

Oh shit. The realization dawned on me that I could very well be pregnant. I went to Boots, bought a stick on which to pee, and saw a plus sign.

Thinking back on it now, it all seems to be such a blur. I panicked for a few days, willing it to not be true. I didn't tell anyone, especially Sophie, who would have started to get all maternal on me, talking about baby showers, and wanting to know how my nausea was. Physically I was feeling great. I didn't have any symptoms. I wasn't nauseous. I peed a little more than normal, but that was it.

I thought about telling Paul. Of course I did. But I wasn't sure myself what I was going to do yet, and I wanted to make some of the decisions without having to deal with a man freaking out, because I was sure that was how he was going to handle it. He had obviously reluctantly had sex with me, it wasn't good, things were awkward and I'd never heard from him again. I wasn't about to pop up now, after two months, and tell him that the condom must have malfunctioned or something. I didn't expect anything from him, and I wasn't even certain that I was going to keep the baby, and so the last thing I wanted was to have to call him up and deal with his reaction on top of my own.

So I spent my workdays focusing on my authors, the books we were releasing, and trying to put out of my mind the grape-sized fetus that was growing in my belly. I knew I had to make some decisions soon, though. Finding out as late as I did - I put myself at about ten to eleven weeks - meant that I was going to have to deal with things with much less time to consider and weigh options than if I had found out after only four weeks.

As it was, fate intervened for me. I suppose. I was sitting at the office on a normal Wednesday afternoon, getting ready for a conference call with the New York office, and I started feeling cramps like a period. They came and went throughout the call, and afterwards when I went to the bathroom there was a tiny streak of red on my knickers.

I numbly went through the rest of my day, took the train home, and sat in a bath, and then called in sick the next day. Two days later, after painfully bleeding clots, the baby passed when I was at home, and I unceremoniously flushed the little bean who had previously lived in my tummy down the toilet. I went to my gynecologist, and they shoved a camera up inside me where they made sure that everything had passed cleanly. I was lucky, they said. I passed everything without needing an operation. Just lots of ibuprofen for pain, and someone to make sure I wasn't feverish.

I should have been relieved. Of course I should have been. I wasn't even sure what I was going to do, in any case. Now the decision had been taken away from me, and I should have felt like a load was taken off my shoulders.

I never told anyone what had happened. Not Sophie, not Paul, no one from work, not even my family. I acted like things were fine. I became incredibly social, flitting from party to party, from club to club, dancing and drinking and acting like I didn't have a care in the world. At night I would climb into bed and curl up into a ball, and talk to the baby-who-almost-was, wondering whether he left because I wasn't sure myself if I was going to keep him.

I felt sure that the baby must have known that I was considering ending its peanut-sized life, and went away because of that. Surely babies know these things, I thought? Something cosmic connects them to the mother's brain. My doctor told me it was impossible, but I knew better. My body had failed me, had listened to the uncertainty in my brain and responded in the only way it knew how - by taking the baby away.

I should have mourned the loss with Enya and candles and meditation, I suppose. That would have been healthier. To process my emotions. I should have started a journal. But I turned to my good friend Jack Daniels, and any warm bodies that could take my mind off the one tiny one I had failed to adequately care for.

That was almost five years ago, and I'm no closer to having a healthy child than I was then. Hell, I can't even manage a healthy relationship with a man long enough to conceive the healthy child.

I blurted all of this out to Matthew, who took it in quietly the way he always seemed to. Nothing phased him. I wondered whether it brought up feelings of loss for his own small baby girl who had died after just a few months on the planet. Had he met her, I wondered?

After that, church and I drifted apart. I stopped going to the regular choral Evensong services that I had loved so much, associating them with Paul. I tried to numb myself, to avoid experiencing the pain I felt over this massive life-changing event, my own tragic story playing out in HD technicolor every night in my dreams, and every day as I walked through Bloomsbury. My only escape was in the books I was editing, the projects I was managing, and then, after hours, keeping myself busy.

What began as accepting every social invitation offered to me (and inviting myself along on ones that weren't) devolved into drinking too much, too often. I have always been a straight laced person, buttoned up and serious about my work; and yet here I was walking down Old Compton Street in high stilettos and a short skirt, half falling over because I was so drunk, clinging to the arm of someone (anyone), trying desperately to capture some of the freedom of youth, but really only refusing to grow up and deal with the heartache I was pushing further and further down.

Which, of course, has led me to this riverbank with my solar powered iphone charger sitting between Matthew and I, stuck in the time of Henry VIII because I was photographed biting a strippers' nipple with a line of coke next to me. I bury my head in my knees and allow a few moments of self pity to wash over me.

Matthew is gentle, as always.

"It doesn't come easily for me to not judge sin," he starts. "Considering that's how I've been raised and all I know, but I do understand what you're saying about everyone thinking their way is right, and I'm trying to listen with an open mind."

I wipe my eyes with my crude layers of dresses and cloaks. The cloth isn't very soft the way my clothes are. What I wouldn't give for a good loom. If I ever get back home, I'm going to put on my clothes every day full of gratitude for modern fabrics. There are a lot of things I'm going to do differently if I get back home, I think.

I take a deep breath. It's odd the way the air here is the same sort of moist cold air that I'm familiar with, but infused with different smells, bugs, and moisture with the additional swampland. I haven't had a drop of modern alcohol in several weeks (mead and ale here truly doesn't count; it's so watered down). The first few days were hard as I was detoxing, but I was also preoccupied with trying to not be discovered as the time traveling imposter that I am. Now I'm over the hump and just miss drinking, but I'm also feeling healthier than I have in years. I can actually breathe the air deeply, pull it into my lungs and experience it. It feels lovely, and I commit to keeping up a life of sobriety when and if I make it home.

CHAPTER THIRTEEN

Breakthrough

The days are getting shorter with the onset of winter, and soon the bells ring for Vespers, calling Matthew away from our little therapy session. He's already missed several prayers today talking with us. But it is no matter, he is learning more things, ideas that are bringing him closer to God, than he would be in Chapel reciting the same Latin prayers. He is going to think and pray and meditate about the things I have told him, he assures me. He walks me back to the dock area where Joseph is waiting (did he go anywhere in town? Do watermen just sit around waiting all day for their passengers?) and it grows dark as we are going home.

Sitting there with Joseph rowing me I realize how vulnerable I have become, how vulnerable women in general are here. He could do something sinister, and no one would hear, and they most likely wouldn't believe me if I told them. Even if they did believe me, it wouldn't matter. It's probably happened before. Fortunately Joseph is a friendly and good man, but I am more keenly aware than ever that if I am going to stay here, I'm going to need some protection beyond Alice. The ideas start to percolate. The thought of marriage is really quite repellent. Even if I did meet someone nice and friendly, what would we talk about? How could I keep a home for him? He probably wouldn't be particularly supportive of me having a career. I'm positive that even the most enlightened men are still not particularly aware of women's equal rights in the workforce.

What if I could make my way on my own? What options could be available to me? Surely there must be women who work somewhere. What about women who have lost their husbands, and carry on their trade. That must be common enough. Especially since I know the future. I have a vision of this sisterhood of economically independent women around me in London. We could start a guild! A women's movement way before its time.

I'm going to need a community around me that loves and protects me, the way our island village protects Alice. People who will care for me when I get sick, for example. I'm going to have to think about it, and maybe talk with Matthew. Perhaps going into a convent might not be a bad idea. I remember that Henry VIII is dissolving many of them, but surely there must be a few that are escaping. Perhaps Matthew will have some ideas.

Still, I need to exhaust all my efforts in figuring out how to get back first. If I can't, then I will move on and think about what to do next. For now, the focus has to be on getting home.

My head is well and truly spent after my long day. The little village seems so welcoming to me now, and I can see the outline of cracks in the shutters at Alice's, meaning she's up with a candle burning, waiting to talk with me. I say goodbye to Joseph and he waits to make sure I'm safely inside before I hear the oars slicing back through the water. When I walk through the door, I see Alice on a chair by the fire, Paddy on her lap with Genny and Tabby on the floor next to her. She's carding some wool, her hands expertly drawing the brush through the wool as she holds it up to the fire. The motion is almost poetic. Paddy is just sleeping, as usual.

She stops her work, and listens while I give her all the details about the day, leaving out the part about the long talk with

Matthew over theology and my history. I'm not sure how she would feel about me talking so openly and honestly with him. She is really excited, though, when she hears of my conversations with Richard Chancellor, and that he is willing to help me.

"You came here once, Natasha, you must be able to get back," is what she says. I keep thinking that to myself too, like a mantra. "It must be nice, knowing that there is a place where you are so at home with so many people who love you," she says next, and it does make me appreciate my home that much more. Even if I never get back, which is a thought almost too awful to consider, I still have a phone full of people who love me that I can look at every day, and remember. Which seems to be more than Alice.

Her talk about the people who love me, and my memories of my decline into, well, I'm not sure what - depravity? sin? separation from God and all that is important to my life? - it makes me long to see home again. London or Los Angeles. Old buildings, cold drizzling rain and ancient water heaters or palm trees, warm sun, and freeways. Somewhere familiar. Somewhere people know and love me. I long to feel known again. And there's so much I want to tell people. I sort of feel like Jimmy Stewart in It's A Wonderful Life. I want to run around telling everyone just how great they are, and how awesome our lives are, and how we should be grateful for so much.

Instead, I mumble something about being tired, and crawl deep under the furs. I take out my freshly charged phone and scroll through pictures while listening to Eric Whitacre on my headphones. I had downloaded Sleep before I left but hadn't listened to it that much. I still felt so pulled towards choral music; I always would, it was my first love. But then it became subsumed with my other love, the unrequited one, the one that made me spiral out of control. I wanted to get back to it. I wanted to have it become part of my life again. One positive side of what had happened was that I could easily fall back in love with my choral music. As long as my solar powered charger kept working, and it had a lifetime guarantee so it should, I could continue to listen to my music. I hadn't shared any of my music with Matthew yet, which I felt was possibly a bit cruel of me, knowing how much he would have loved it, and loved knowing that it was available. But there were things I wasn't ready to share yet, and music was one of them.

I was warm under the furs with the rain swirling around outside, little drops coming through the thatch, and down the fireplace, splashing me from time to time, though I stayed close to it anyway because it was better than the wind that was coming through the cracks around the doorway. Alice was in her bed. I really must introduce her to rope beds. I remember going to museums on the east coast when I was a kid, seeing historic houses like Monticello, and they always had these rope bottom beds with the mattresses over top of them. I was thinking that rope couldn't be that hard to come by, if they had it in the colonial days. What was it made of, anyway? Fiber of some sort?

Then I thought back to the book I had read about Richard Chancellor, and how rope was one of the things that he had brought back from Russia that had made trade between England and Russia so important. And it all comes full circle, I thought. Alice wouldn't have rope bottom beds until Richard Chancellor went to Russia, and he couldn't go to Russia until I gave him all my knowledge so that he could be an amazing sea captain who would have such a brilliant reputation that he would be recruited for this major voyage of exploration. So really, I was to thank for rope bottom beds. But, how could that be, considering they must have existed in order for me to see them in museums? And this was the point at which time my head would start spinning.

I pulled Paddy to me, despite the fact that he really wanted to play with my headphones, and hugged him close. He struggled at first, and then he finally gave in and started purring. I scrolled through my pictures, talking to him. "Look Paddy, this is my mother." A picture of me when I went back home last Christmas. Christmas in Los Angeles. With the fake snow at Disneyland. The road trip to Lake Arrowhead with real snow, and sliding down the mountain in giant inner tubes. The sunset at the beach with the bonfire at Dockweiler, watching planes take off over the ocean while eating In and Out burgers surrounded by friends from when I was young. People who knew me when I was still full of life, and before I became a wreck.

I really need to get over the fact that I've become a wreck, and start seeing myself differently. I think about Louise Hay, the author I read who believes that you can cure yourself of all sorts of ailments merely through your thoughts. She's a little new age-y for me, but I do agree with her statement that your power always comes from the present moment. We can't do anything about the past, except live out the consequences of our thoughts and actions based on those thoughts. The future is given by our thoughts today. So starting today, starting now, I need to start thinking good thoughts about myself. After all, I am no longer a wreck right now in this moment. Hell, I am using knowledge I forgot I even had to influence a man who would become a great sea captain and discover a route to Russia. Not bad for a drunk.

I keep going through my phone, looking at the books I've downloaded, wishing there were more. At least I have my ipad, too. I always have been obsessed with having a lot of books with me whenever I go away, a holdover from a family driving vacation in Maine where I ran out of Ramona Quimby books to read and had to stare at trees for 16 hours. I vowed I would never be without books again, and so I am like a sherpa carrying my books around. At least with the gadgets my bag isn't quite as heavy as when I would carry three paperbacks with me. Still, I think I'll probably make it through all the books I have with me in this lifetime if I never get back, which makes me sad.

I've been keeping my phone in airplane mode with most of my apps completely off so as not to waste battery, but I decide to indulge a little bit now that I know the solar charger works so well. I play some Candy Crush, and do a little crossword puzzle before shutting down those apps. And then, just for fun, I decide to see what would happen if I turned off airplane mode. Because I'm now 500 years before satellites and cell phone towers, I'm sure that I'll just get a message like I do when I'm in a plane flying over a large city and think I might be able to snag a faint signal and send a quick text message (I seriously don't believe that my trying to find a signal could interfere with the radar of the plane. I mean, come on, if it were that dangerous, the times when people forgot to put their phones in airplane mode, or turn them off, would be totally life threatening, and I just don't see that happening. I think it's just another way the TSA makes life miserable for us when we're traveling).

So I press the button to confirm that I'm turning airplane mode off, and then watch as it tries to find a signal. I don't know why I want to do it. Just to torture myself, I suppose. Another form of masochism. Remind myself just how stuck and separate I really am.

Except.

Except...

Bars appear. Three of them. Holy Sweet Jesus in Heaven! I have a signal! I have three distinct bars. Holy crap. I have three bars! I gasp. Paddy groans, angry at me for disrupting his leisure. I get out of bed and run over to Alice. "Alice, you've gotta see this, I have three bars!" she has already fallen asleep, and looks at me as if it's gibberish, which of course it is to her. But it means I could make a call. Or go on Facebook. Or buy more books.

But then the bigger picture hits me.

What it really means is that all time is concurrent, like a curtain with ripples in it. It's all happening at once, like the way so many science fiction writers, and physicists believe. How else could I have a signal if the satellites weren't already in the sky? My time, the time of cell phones and Frappuccinos, is happening right now, right this very minute, and I just wound up getting caught in a fold.

The ramifications of all of this are swirling around through my head. My time is happening right now, even while I'm here at King's. It's all happening at the same time. Time is just an imaginary construct.

"Alice, I need to get to Matthew. Do you think I could go now? Could you take me?"

Alice looks at me like I'm insane. "You can't go into King's at night like this. You could be arrested."

"But surely when I tell them I'm there to see Matthew, he'll come out and help?"

She just grunts. "Don't put all your faith in Matthew."

"Alice, just watch this."

I dial the number of my mom, and put the phone on speaker. It's 8 hours earlier in LA. She should be at the gym. Or something. Who even knows. But either way, it starts ringing. "Hey honey!" I hear, clear as day, right here in this hut.

Alice screams and moves as far away from the phone as she can. "It talks! It's possessed!"

"Alice, shut up. Hey mama. I just wanted to say hi."

"Sweetie, we've been worried. We haven't heard from you in ages, and then we heard you weren't showing up for work, you have no idea how worried we were. And there was that awful picture. I thought maybe you were so upset about it, and did something, well, even worse."

So I did miss my meeting with Howard. Well, I can't worry about that right now. I have other things I need to deal with. I consider calling him to explain what happened. Like, hey there, sorry I didn't come to work. I'm stuck in the space time continuum. It wouldn't be the craziest excuse ever, I guess.

"No, mama, I'm fine. Just a bit hung up with stuff right now. Can you let everybody know I'm ok? I gotta go, ok. I just wanted to say bye before I went to bed."

"Bed? It's only like eight there, isn't it?"

"Right, I meant dinner." Of course, people in London in 2015 don't go to bed at eight.

"Sure thing sweetie. Thanks for letting me know you're ok. Hey I put a package in the mail to you, ok? Make sure you look for it. There's Hershey's chocolate in there. I don't want it to melt sitting outside." As if chocolate could melt sitting outside in London in November. She forgets that her sun doesn't exist for me between November and March.

"Ok mama, I'll look out for it. I gotta go. Love you. Lots."

I hang up and Alice is curled up on the edge of her bed staring at me in fear with huge eyes and a look of utter panic. "You really are from the future."

"What did you think?"

"I'm not really sure. I didn't think you were lying, and you certainly have lots of things that show you're not from here, but...I just didn't know..."

"Yes, Alice, I really am from the future, and I just talked to my mom there. How can I get a message to Matthew, do you think? I know you'll know how," I look at her meaningfully.

"Ok, you can get a waterman to take a message. It's not safe for you to go. Write something down and I'll take it over to Henry Robinson and he will take it to Matthew. He's my friend."

I write down something cryptic but clearly showing I need to speak with him. Damn, I wish I could just text him. Now, knowing that I could if only he had a cell phone makes it even more frustrating.

"Huge development. Can you get Richard Chancellor to meet back there tomorrow?" is what I write.

Alice runs out into the dark night, carrying my piece of vellum out to her friend Henry with a coin for his time. He will get it there as soon as he can, he promises, when the fog lifts and it's safe to venture into the waters.

CHAPTER FOURTEEN

Music of the Spheres

So now all I can do is wait. But waiting has never been so much fun. I have a very strong signal, and so we stay up all night, with me demonstrating for Alice all the wonders of the internet. We are like giddy girls at a slumber party, playing with our new toy. Of course, I'm more giddy. She is astounded.

Since she is interested in health, I show her articles on germs, antibiotics, and YouTube videos showing births with epidurals. I download more music from Spotify, and we share my headset while I show her videos of kittens, because you can never have too many kitten videos. Then we download more books and magazines, and finally I show her Facebook.I have over two thousand notifications, which makes me both pleased that I am still so loved, and a bit nauseous because everyone seems to miss me so much.

"You must not get a lot of work done in the future, if everybody has these distractions all the time," she observes.

"Yep, it's totally hard to concentrate. Our brains are all going to mush." And I smile. "But look what we've been able to do..." and I show her a video of the moon landing. Then we look at a model of the solar system. I'm pretty much in awe of how much information is available to me now, having been without it for three weeks and seeing life through 16th century eyes.

Then, because I can't resist, I check my work email. There are literally dozens of messages from Howard asking where the hell I am. Sophie wondering whether I took the "escape to the country" thing a little too literally. And other staff members needing things from me. I hit "delete" on all of them.

I really just can't be bothered. I want to get back home. And once I'm home, I'll figure out what next, but I'm getting really clear on the fact that I need to make some serious changes in my life, and having a high stress job where I have become an alcoholic can't be good for my soul. I need to meditate more. That's pretty much the only thing I know about my life when I get home. There will be more meditation.

Alice wants to know the immediate future, what will happen with the religious reforms, and who will succeed Henry. I'm not sure how I feel about sharing all of this with her. It dawns on me, for example, that Richard Chancellor could check on himself and see what's going to happen, and alter the course of history, which I don't want to happen. I could wind up setting in motion a whole bunch of changes that could entirely screw up history. I'm going to need to tread lightly. Not divulge too much. Suddenly all the pressure and weight of what I could do here is weighing on me. It's like I hold the future of the world in the palm of my hand. Talk about high stress.

"Alice, I don't know. I don't know whether I should show you any of this, really. What if it somehow messes up the trajectory? I mean, I know what happens to Richard Chancellor. How can I show him that? Won't it make things so hard for him to try to not change his fate?"

"But if it's fate, surely it can't be altered?" she asks.

That, my friend, is the million dollar question.

"I don't know Alice. I have no idea. I don't know that anyone has done this before. If they have, I haven't heard about it. I haven't seen the rulebook."

She's quiet for a moment. "the wheel of fortune decides our fate, doesn't it? Sometimes we are up, and then just as quickly we are down. We can't fight that. If it's meant to be, if God decrees it, then there's no way we can change it."

"But Alice, what if I told you that you were going to die tomorrow by drowning in the River Cam. Wouldn't you avoid the Cam all together?"

"No, not really. I know this life is but a stepping stone to something bigger. I believe that. If it's my time to go, I would hope that it would be quick and that someone would take care of the cats, but I've led a good life and felt love, and for that I'm grateful."

I am dumbfounded by her answer. Really, she wouldn't try to change it? No, she really wouldn't.

I think about whether to let Chancellor know what happens to him. I know he dies off the coast of Scotland in a shipwreck, but that he died saving the life of the first Russian ambassador, who went on to help start trading negotiations with England, which was the nascent beginnings of the British Empire. He had a huge role to play in history. Maybe if I framed it that way, it's something that he would have been willing to die for. But at the same time, if he knew the storm was coming, maybe he would have sought out land sooner. What would I do, walking towards the inevitability of what fate had thrown my way, I wonder. Could I be as strong and peaceful about it as Alice thinks she would, trusting that the afterlife would hold something for me that would make this life just a short preparation for it? Or what if I knew that my life and death would play a role in the history of my country? Would I be able to go forward with fate then?

These are all deeply philosophical questions that I wish I could talk over with someone. But I can't. The only people who know the whole truth about me are steeped in their belief systems, and for them it is capital-T Truth. I wonder where the skeptics are. If they even exist. I think about the timing of it all again. The Enlightenment doesn't really take shape in England for another century. No, critical thinking about the universe doesn't really seem to exist yet. I'm sure that somewhere, maybe London, there is a skeptic who would love to talk philosophy with me, but most people have grown up accepting the teachings of the church as infallible, and are completely sure that their life here is just practice for the glorious eternity in heaven that awaits them if they behave. That, I suppose, must be why all of the religious dissension of the Protestant Reformation makes it so difficult for ordinary people, who are finding their lives turned upside down.

I will leave the philosophizing for the clerics and scholars, sadly. All I can do is curl up with Alice and fall asleep, waiting for word from Matthew. It comes in the form of a messenger who arrives before sunrise, banging at the door, with a note from Matthew inviting me to visit his chambers this afternoon after nonne. He'll send Joseph with a boat. It's still raining, and I'm not sure how, or whether, I'll be able to charge my phone today, so I decide to keep it turned off until I can show it to Matthew and Richard.

We get up and start to bake some hard bread for the day. Alice gets the porridge going over the fire, as the raindrops continue to drip in and sizzle on the fire. We won't be going out to work in the garden today, but Alice is worried about some of the plants, so she runs out quickly and pull up the root vegetables that are ready so they don't rot. That means we'll be having more carrots and onions tonight.

She also checks the thatch in the roof to make sure it's not catching fire. Unbelievably, she tells me that many fires start in thatch during the rain because people grow less careful, the thatch gets moved around and disrupted, and the little animals that burrow around in there move things. So she makes sure that everything is in order. Meanwhile I stand sentry waiting for her to come back in, holding a giant blanket to wrap her up in. She's soaked and coughing, and I worry about her catching cold, but she just shakes her head at me and wrings out her garments and blows her nose on her skirt.

"Seriously Alice, can you at least let your clothes dry by the fire and wear a blanket in the house until then? It's really not good. I know more about this than you do. Please." She smiles at me and reluctantly lets me dry her off and wrap the blanket around her while I lay her clothes out to dry in the warmth. I know enough to know that colds can be fatal in the 16th century, and I don't want either one of us getting one. It's very warm and cozy in most of our little cottage, and the smoke is exiting through the hole in the roof just as it's meant to be, rather than filling up our space.

At the appointed time I start to bundle myself up in Alice's woolen cape, and multiple layers of clothing to try to stay warm in the boat to Matthew's. She gives me her leather hat, which should keep my head dry, and I wrap my phone up in the other spare strip of leather I have, and put it in my bra. I seem to be ready for the elements, but I am not looking forward to stepping outside. The ground isn't really ground at all, but simply mush. It kills me that I have amazingly warm boots just inside, and I can't wear them. But I am consoled by the fact that Alice is wearing them around the house since it doesn't appear that anyone is going to just be stopping in on a day like this. At least someone is wearing them.

And back up the river I go, sloshing around, getting soaked. Joseph just stares straight ahead, not even trying to make conversation, looking stoic as the rain drips off his hat onto his drenched clothing. I am daydreaming about Matthew's fireplace, and a nice warm mug of mead when we get to King's and I step out of the boat, and again Matthew comes out to greet me, covering me in his cape and thick hat that covers my face so that no one can see me. He bundles me down the hallway to his rooms again, and as I am disrobing and trying to warm up, I see that Chancellor is already there, warming himself by the fire.

"What a horrible day," I say, by way of greeting. I settle myself down with a piece of nice wheat bread, some apples, and a mug of warm ale, and then they both look at me expectantly.

"Ok you guys," I start out, drifting back into modern parlance. "Here's what I've found out." I explain how I realized that I have a signal on my phone, and how I was able to call my mother.

"I still have over half the battery left. I can do it again." They both kind of look at me blankly.

"Don't you get what this means?" More blank stares, and not for the first time I sort of curse the late medieval thought processes. "It means that all time is happening at once, just like the theories say. The satellites are there. You just don't know about them yet because your time didn't launch them."

There's dead silence in the room as they take in what I just told them. "Don't you see, you guys. It's like a curtain or a piece of cloth with wrinkles and folds." I think about any kind of language I can use to make it sound more plausible. The fact that they can't comprehend it is maddening to me, but of course they can't yet. How else can I put it. "It's all happening at one time. We're all in our own folds, only I somehow got mismatched and I'm now in your fold. Something happened at that Evensong service the other week, and I wound up back here, but my time is still going on. Do you want me to call my mom again?"

They stare at me, uncomprehending.

"Look," I pull up the internet. "look at this map of the world. Look at Amazon.com. Look, this is the news." I pull up the Guardian's site. "Look at the date. November 20, 2015. It's happening today. This is the news of today, but almost 500 years from now."

Matthew takes my phone and looks at the screen, staring at it in disbelief. "Surely it must be some kind of spell, or something." He starts to look suspiciously at me. I sigh.

"Matthew, really. Do I have to go over this with you, too? Is Edward starting to get to you? There's no spell. There's nothing except for me being caught here."

Chancellor has been silent, strumming his fingers on the arm of his chair with one hand, and stroking his beard with the other. "So your time is happening now, and you just made a switch to this time... but they're all happening at one time?"

"I think that's the only answer, given that I have a cell phone signal."

"So is the time of Christ happening now," Chancellor asks. "The Romans? If so, where are they, why can't I see them?"

"You guys and your logic," I sigh. "Because it's like a different dimension or something." I explain dimensions to them. Two dimensional. Three dimensional. Maybe the fourth dimension is the ability to go back in time. They still look incredibly skeptical.

"How else do you explain the fact that I have a signal on my phone?"

"Magic?" comes the response from Matthew.

"Matthew. There is no such thing as Magic. You know this. Stop giving me answers like that." I am losing patience with this man.

An argument ensues over the validity of Magic. Matthew wants to know how else I can explain the moon landing if not for Magic. I tell him it's physics, and maybe before his people understood physics Magic could have been an appropriate thought, but once we got the idea of force and acceleration and mass and all of those Newtonian equations, Magic went out the door, except for at birthday parties and carnivals.

To prove my point I show him the youtube video of the Moon Landing.

"Physics," I say, at the end, smugly. "If it was just magic, you'd have done it already. Nope, it's Physics." Next I google Newton and make them both read about him.

Chancellor suddenly speaks up. "Ok, so in theory all time is happening at the same time. This Moon Landing is happening right now? Everything is happening right now. Only we just don't know it because we are in our own time."

Praise the lord, he gets it!

I nod.

"And somehow you got plucked from your time and have wound up here, in our time. But your time is still going on."

"As evidenced by all the emails of my company wondering where I am, yes."

"So we need to figure out how you can get back. Since you got here once."

Finally!

"I'm going to have to think about this more, Natasha," Chancellor finishes up. "It's a lot to throw at someone."

I have a lightbulb moment that might appeal to their thought processes.

"Look, I'm not saying that the spiritual realm had nothing to do with it. Let's look at when I arrived. It was November 1. The day after Halloween, when the idea is that the spirits all come out to play, right? Maybe something strange happened with a combination of the music, and the spirits still being out, and everything like that. I mean, maybe there was just some giant perfect storm of all the elements that I wound up right smack dab in the middle of. But all I know is that my time is still happening now, and I really want to get back to it."

"Sophie, what was the music that was being sung at the time that you fainted and woke up here?" Matthew is stroking his chin.

"Oh, it was this beautiful O Magnum Mysterium by Morten Lauridsen. Just heaven," I start gushing over it, and then look on my phone to see if I can pull it up and play it for them.

Matthew looks nonplussed. "Bit strange to have a Christmas piece being sung on All Saint's Day," he says. "The church really must be changing if that is allowed to happen."

I shush him as I find it on Spotify, and I think that it's finally time to introduce Matthew to the wonders of Recorded Music. I press play and as the opening chords start up, his face becomes ashen, his mouth caught in a little O and his eyes fixed on the phone.

"Is that music playing now?"

"Sort of. I mean, it's a recording. Oh, it doesn't matter. Yes, it's playing. This is what the choir was singing when I came here."

He sits, transfixed. It's like his whole world has just been turned upside down. That's sort of how I felt the first time I heard choral music from his time, so I can only imagine how he must be feeling. We sit and grin at each other, and he bends down to be even closer to the speaker. I pull out my headphones and plug them in, showing him how to put them in his ears. This way he'll have a better sound quality, and he can be really consumed by the music.

Meanwhile Richard is stroking his beard.

"Natasha," he starts, "what do you know about the Music of the Spheres?"

"Not very much other than having heard the term," is my response.

"I just wonder..." Richard looks over at Matthew, whose eyes are closed, and who is in a state of complete choral music bliss.

I reach over and grab the phone, keeping the music going, but quickly google Music of the Spheres. The idea that celestial bodies somehow are musical in their rotations.

"I don't know that much, and we would have to consult an expert, but I wonder whether we just happened to be at the precise moment in the rotation of the planets that a harmony you heard was in alignment with the planets, and that, combined with the day it was, somehow caused your wrinkle to unfold, as it were."

It sounds as plausible as anything else I've heard.

"We would need to get a scholar involved," Richard says. "That means telling more people. And we should get a copy of the music you were listening to. Do you think you could write it down?" He starts to get really excited, dictating things. "It would be good to see the harmonies and match it up with what we know of the planetary alignment."

Only thing is, Renaissance England doesn't know anything about the planetary alignment compared to what modern England does. I think maybe this is something for MI5 or some government organization. When I share this thought with them, he looks disappointed.

"But we can help," Richard says. "We can consult astrologers."

"All of whom predicted that each of the King's children would be healthy boys, right?"

He looks put in his place.

I think I need to call someone in my time. Someone I can trust to not think I'm crazy. Someone who will take me seriously and help me with this. Someone who will know who to call. Someone who has their hand on the pulse and knows what's going on. Someone like... Sophie.

"I'm going to call my friend. If you are going to start consulting experts here, I need to have people on the ground for me, too. Matthew, music time is over for right now." At least I wait until the song is over, and then press pause, and pull the ear buds from him.

"That was the most divine thing, truly God speaks to us all in such glorious ways..." and on and on and on he gushes. I do love his enthusiasm. But I have other things on my mind right now.

I dial Sophie's number. It's after work, she should be home.

CHAPTER FIFTEEN

The Plan Develops

"Natasha, finally, for the love of God, I know I told you to go away and turn your phone off, but what the hell is happening with you? Where the hell are you?"

I really miss my friend.

"Ok, Sophie. Look, I don't have a lot of time. You're on speaker phone with Matthew and Richard."

"Have you been kidnapped and you're being held for ransom?? Do I need to call the police?"

"Well, no, and yes. You'd better sit down. Because I'm going to tell you something that might make you freak out a little bit."

"Well, I was in the middle of feeding fish fingers to the munchkins, but they can survive on their own for a second. Let me go into the bedroom. Listen you two, do not throw food at each other. If there is any food on the ground when I come back out, even a crumb, so help me God, I will take away your electronics for a week. Ok, I'm going up the stairs now. Talk to me."

"Sophie, I've become stuck somewhere. I'm in Cambridge."

"Oh Cambridge is beautiful. There are some lovely shops there around the colleges, and you must go punting," suddenly she sounds really distracted. "But what are you doing there, and why have you been out of touch for so long?"

"Well, yes, the thing is, I have been doing a lot of punting. But I'm not in the Cambridge that you know."

"Massachusetts?"

"No, Cambridge England. Circa 1539."

"Well, yeah, it's so historic there. Are you staying in a college? And why haven't you called anyone? It's really irresponsible of you to just go away like this. We were so worried. Howard is so bleeping mad at you. You have no idea."

"No, Sophie. I have traveled back in time. I am literally in 1539."

Dead silence. Then.

"Don't you dare screw with me you irresponsible alcoholic. You have no idea the tale I'm spinning to explain your absence, and then you throw this pile of crap at me?"

"Nice to know how you really feel. But I'm telling you the truth. I told you it might sound weird. I did as you said. I packed a bag and I went away for a weekend. I even got a room at a bed and breakfast. I was turning over a new leaf, reading new books and I was going to start meditating. I thought a good start would be to go to Evensong service at King's. I'd never been."

Silence. Then, "I'm still listening."

"It was November 1, right? And midway through, I felt really dizzy. I was getting upset wondering what my life had come to, how things had turned out so miserably, everything like that. And then all of a sudden, I leaned my head forward, and I fainted. When I woke up, Brother Matthew here was leaning over me. He's been helping me. I've been staying in the fens with a lovely woman called Alice."

"Wait, let me get this straight. You are living in the 16th century with a woman called Alice, and you fainted and this happened?"

"Yep."

"How are you calling me?"

"See, that's the thing, Sophie!" I'm glad she came around to the subject right away. "I had assumed I wouldn't have any service, so I turned my phone on airplane mode. I had that cool solar charger you gave me from the camping trip to Cornwall, right? So I could access my pictures and music and stuff. But then last night, just for giggles, I turned on the phone to see what would happen, and there were three bars. Three bars, Sophie! I had a signal!"

"So it's true then."

"Are you thinking what I think you're thinking?"

"You know, what science fiction books say. That all time is happening at once. Concurrent time or something like that."

"Oh Thank you! You get it! These jokers here have no idea what I'm talking about." I'm so relieved.

"Well they wouldn't, would they?" she responds.

"They've been very nice to me," I feel a need to stick up for my new friends.

"Yes, but they didn't discover calculus."

Matthew and Richard look a little offended.

"Well, they are in the city where Newton discovered it?" I suggest, making it seem a little more like they have something to do with it, and that makes their chests puff out a little bit more.

"So here's the thing, Sophie. I need you to do some research for me. I came to Evensong service at King's on November 1, All Saint's Day. The music playing when I lost consciousness was by Morten Lauridsen, a contemporary composer. I looked him up and he's based out of the University of Southern California. These guys here have brought up the idea of the music of the spheres. I need you to research it. It's some idea that the planets rotating make some kind of perfect mathematical music. And their thought is that maybe there was some kind of harmony or something, right at the very time that the planets were in their rotation or whatever, and I just happened to be in the right place for it to cause me to get stuck in this wrinkle and wind up back here. Can you do some research for me on it?"

Sophie is silent, and I can tell she's writing things down.

"Tasha, don't you think that this is maybe something for, I don't know, like the government or something?"

"See, that's what they're saying here, too, but Sophie, think about it. If people find out about this, like more than the few of us who do - Matthew, Richard Chancellor, Alice, and now you - all of history could get really seriously screwed up. I mean, if there truly is something to what they're saying, then what if people start to abuse it. Something like this couldn't be kept secret forever, Sophie. People would start to mess with it. Even if it wasn't now, even if it was a hundred or two hundred years from now, and somebody found a record of it in a drawer somehow, and started messing with history, that would be bad. We aren't meant to be going back and forth like this. It's cool that I'm back here seeing all this and everything, but I seriously don't want to stay here, and I don't think other people should be playing around with it."

"But if somebody did start to mess around with it, wouldn't we know, because it would have been recorded?"

"Ok, Sophie, now you're just screwing around with my brain, which is really not cool."

"I'm serious though. People would have recorded strange visitors, no?"

"There are so many different places we could go with this, Sophie. What if the CIA is doing it all the time, and we just don't know about it? What if there was a covert operation to kill Kennedy that didn't work the first time and people from the future went back and did it the second time properly? What if Cleopatra was really killed by some guy in 2800 who went back in time and messed with the entire Peloponnesian War because the first time around Egypt became the ruler of the world for eternity, and he was still a slave, building pyramids, and he figured it out and went back, and all of history as we're living it is only happening this way because someone else altered it from the future?"

"Woah. That is crazy. Hey! Benjamin Noah! I told you! No food on the floor! Tasha, my time is running short here. First, let me think of something to tell Howard. Second, let me do some research into this music of the spheres thing. How should I get in touch with you?"

"I have the solar charger you gave me, but it's super rainy here and it's not like I can just have it out charging because people would see and think I was a witch...seriously...so I have to be kind of discreet with my charging, and that's tough. Also, there are a lot of animals. And manure. And the fens haven't been drained yet, so everything is very wet."

"It sounds miserable."

"Oh Sophie, my God, it is. The cloth! The homespun cloth! It itches like crazy! And there are literally mice and bugs, like, everywhere. I am just used to them now. I'm freaking sleeping on straw. And even though I have my warm boots with me, I can't use them because they would show everyone I was a foreigner, so I have these ugly leather wraps around my feet. And the leather was a cow last month."

"Crap, Tasha. God, we've got to get you back. You aren't meant for this."

"At least Alice is lovely. And she has cats. One of them snuggles with me every night and keeps the mice in my straw bed away. And she has a nice thatched roof. She lives in a little village that's about a 20 minute ride away by boat. I think it's east. I need to google map it now that I have a signal. Anyway, it doesn't really matter. For the moment I'm warm, and I'm fed, and I have people here who are helping me, so it's all good. I think if you text me, that would be best. Eats up less battery. And Sophie...can you look into some monk here called Edward? He almost called me a witch the night I arrived. I'm a little worried about him."

At this Matthew sits forward. "I told him that you were ill, and part of a band of pilgrims, and had left. He believed it."

"Who was that?"

"That's Matthew."

"Hey Matthew. Thanks for looking out for our girl. She needs all the help she can get."

"It's my honor. I am looking forward to hearing more of the wonders of your time, and further messages from the Lord with gratitude for the wondrous ways in which he speaks to us."

"Ok then. So I'm going to research the music of the spheres. Get hold of this Lauridsen music if I can. And look into some guy called Edward who was a monk or scholar or something at King's. Easy peasy. I really gotta go before they kill each other. Look, can you text me every day or so to let me know you're ok? We're going to figure something out, Tasha. I promise you we will. You got yourself there. We will get you back, all of us working together, ok?"

I start to tear up. I love my friends. This is just so sad.

"And if we can't, then at least I can text you all the updates here. You know, reality TV and other important things. As long as you don't drop your phone in the river."

I sign off giving her my love, and she's going to think about what to tell Howard and the team, and text me tomorrow.

When I hang up I sit the phone on my lap and just stare at it for a little while. It's bittersweet, being able to talk to people from home. I love it, and I wouldn't trade it for the world, but before I knew I could do that, it didn't really seem so real. I could sort of imagine that the whole world had ended or something. But talking to my mom, and Sophie, brings it back to me how much I miss them, and how lost I am. It's an odd sort of being lost because I know exactly where I am. I'm only about 60 miles from London. Heck, I could probably walk there and see my neighborhood.

But I'm lost in time, and that's so much worse. I think of Sophie in her home in Notting Hill, near the Ladbroke Grove station, across the street from a 19th century gothic-revival church, making dinner and talking to her family after the long day. I think about the rest of her street, hugging their families, and preparing their meals, and drying off from the rain, and soaking in bathtubs, and all of the things that people do and take for granted. God, what I wouldn't give for a bath right now. With some trashy magazine like Heat or Look or something like that.

I sit in silence and listen to the fire, and the rain - the never ending relentless rain - on the window panes. At least we have window panes here. Alice's cottage doesn't have glass, and the windows just have wooden shutters that go across them to keep the cold and rain out. Or to try to keep the cold and rain out. I miss my central heating. If I started thinking about all the things I miss I'd just lose it so I take a deep breath. Matthew does too.

"Was it hard, talking to her?"

"What do you think?" I respond.

"Natasha, I believe that God has sent you here for a reason, both for you, and for us. I have been praying, and I really think that this wasn't any accident. We need you. And you need us. For whatever reason we can't figure out yet. We just need to be patient. And when the time is right, we'll get you back to your home."

Chancellor begs his leave then as well. "I'm going to go to London soon anyway. There is a merchant from Bristol I am meeting. While I am there, I will go to the Guildhall, and do a bit of searching to find someone who is an expert in the planetary motions and the music of the spheres. We may be onto something with that. It's at least a way to start looking."

"Richard, is it Sebastian Cabot you're meeting?"

"No, he's in Spain still. It's someone who knows him though, who works with his company there. Why?"

"Have you met with them before?"

"No, they just contacted me. They heard that I've been studying here, learning mathematics, and navigation, and wanted to ask me my thoughts about a potential new route to the Indies."

"The route North, right?"

"How did you know?"

"Richard, you forget, I know because it already happened and I've read books about it. The northeast passage through Russia. You're going to meet the czar of Russia."

"So it's going to be a successful voyage?"

I think about the fact that two ships were lost and the men died on board, and the fact that Richard himself would die three years later. But for him, and for England, it was successful in the short term, so I respond with a simple, "yes."

He lets out a sigh. "That is so good to hear."

"What can I tell you that will help you get the job?" I ask. "I already know you will get it, of course. But if there's anything I can do, or tell you."

"The map of the world you drew me was so helpful. And showing me the globes on your device. No one right now knows what the world looks like."

"And for all intents and purposes, neither do you. Be clever, Richard. Be clever enough to get the job, but not too clever to give away your knowledge."

"Indeed, Madam, and I thank you. I shall research as much as I can on these thoughts, and return to you with information in the next fortnight."

He goes, leaving Matthew and I alone.

"You know, I don't think you need to worry about Edward," Matthew says.

"There was something sinister in his face, Matthew. I don't trust it. You know, I always knew that people - women - were more vulnerable in the past. But until living it, you can't really imagine it."

"What do you mean? Surely women are protected?"

"Yes, women who fit into your box of what is appropriate for them. But what about the older women, the widows. Or those who are unmarried. What about women who don't want to get married? Who want a career? You know, in my day, there's this thing called women's rights. Women can vote. Women can get jobs. They don't need to have a husband. They can have careers and support themselves. It's all very liberating. If women did that here, and had animals for company, they'd be branded as witches. I understand, looking back on it historically, in an age when communication was difficult, people needed to stick together in their community and live by their reputations, and if you left and went somewhere else to have an adventure or reinvent yourself or something you were seen as suspicious. But you really don't know what to do with people who don't fit into your worldview, do you?"

I'm actually starting to get a little riled up. It's the frustration of missing home, of being alone here, of talking to my friend and missing her, all of it is just combining to make me really upset at this century in particular, and anything pre 1960's women's lib in general.

"If I was who I am in this century, I'd be burned. So yeah, I'm afraid of Edward."

Matthew is quiet.

"So in your time, women don't need to have the protection of men?"

"Nope."

"Is there still violence? Against women?"

"Of course, but women can fight back. Correct me if I'm wrong, but here it's not called rape if a man forces himself on his wife, right? Women have very few rights."

Matthew is quiet. "I know it must be hard for you, Natasha."

"It is. And the worst thing is, I really want to take advantage of this adventure. You know, it's the definition of a once in a lifetime opportunity. I want to go out and explore. I want to see Cambridge. I know Cambridge. I've had meetings with authors here a few times. I would love to figure out how to get to London. But then I remember. I'm a woman and women probably can't travel alone in this time period. And anyway, London is what, like 60 miles away. That's not just an hour train ride like it is for me in my century. So I'm bummed because there's all this amazing stuff I would love to see, and I can't, because I'm a freaking woman who shouldn't be here and there's a monk who's suspicious of me. You know, I would love to come to a choral service here. You can't even imagine how awesome that would be for me. To hear music sung the way it was originally in the original setting. I go to Evensong services at Westminster Abbey all the time. At least, I did, before I started turning into an alcoholic. But anyway, I would love to see a service here. But I can't. Because I'm a common woman and they don't let common women into those services, do they? We can't even have equal access to God."

"Stay this evening," Matthew says.

I laugh.

"No, I'm serious. I will put a robe over you, and you will keep your head down. You can be a pilgrim. No one will notice."

I look up at him. "Do you think so?"

"I know so. And besides, Edward isn't even here. He's had to go to Ely to take some papers to the Bishop there. There are so many changes going on, Sophie. Your world has fallen apart, but you know, for many of us in the monastic orders, our lives have fallen apart too. Who will provide hospitality and medical treatment for the poor when the monasteries are fully dissolved. Wealthy men will buy the land, and no one will think about the good that the monks and nuns do. And what of the brothers and sisters themselves? Who will look out for them. And what's worse, even saying these things is treasonous now. We can't even talk about it amongst ourselves because we don't know who we can trust, or who will run to Cromwell or something."

"But I thought you supported the Dissolution? You seem so liberal. And you know Cromwell?"

"In theory I do. I really do. I think they are, often, a snakepit of corruption, and as an institution the whole thing is evil. But, with that said, many of them do very good work. The vast majority of the individuals in the orders are fine people who are trying to follow God. The vast majority of village priests are doing their best with what they are given. But the people at the top are destroying it for everyone. Those are the people who should be dealt with."

"Sounds like politics in my time, too. There's a saying...the more things change the more they stay the same."

Matthew laughs, stands up, and tosses a robe to me. "Here you go. Service starts in about 45 minutes. With this robe on, you can easily go anywhere in the city if you want. Just keep your head down."

CHAPTER SIXTEEN

Evensong Service Take Two

The rain is letting up a bit, so the idea of a wander through the city and colleges is appealing. I put the robe on, and am magically transformed into a member of the college. No one bats an eyelash at me in the scholar's robe, and I walk over to Parker's Piece, through the little courtyards where I know that in my time there's a Mark's and Spencer food hall. What I wouldn't give for some chocolate rolls from M&S. A tub of chocolate rolls. All gooey and decadent. Keep focused, Tasha. Do not be distracted by chocolate fantasies.

It all looks so different. So rural. But I know that Cambridge is a great university city, even now. I see the building going on at Trinity. I know it's a market town. But it's all so depressing and lonely to me. I miss the constant energy of a big city. I miss feeling like part of civilization. This just feels like backcountry farmyards. Cows literally are wandering down the street. I thought that was just a market day phenomenon, but nope, it seems to happen all the time. I hop around cow shit and land on a dead goat. Seriously, what is wrong with this city and these people. Haven't they heard about germs yet? No, of course they haven't. I really want some Purell.

The walk is doing me good, though. The rhythm of my feet, combined with seeing different views; it does something for me. I've always thrived on having some variation in my life. In my time, I do it through travel, parties, and anonymous hookups like I'm some kind of college kid. But here that's not really an option, and anyway, I need to edit that list. I could substitute books and music for parties and hookups.

As I walk, I look around at the people. The streets are full of people walking around the dead goat just like me. Common looking women wearing homespun brown clothing, walking with their children. Men going into a tavern, just like they do now, only without the football on tv. They probably get drunk and cheer about other things. Like which cow had the most milk this morning. Who knows. I take them all in, these people who are alive right now, who are part of this bustling community of shops and colleges, but will be dead in the next fifty years.

After about 30 minutes of wandering I walk back over to King's, feeling really excited at the prospect of seeing a service from the 1530's. I'm a little worried because I'm not sure what kind of service it will be. I'm trying to remember where we are in the cycle. The Book of Common Prayer hasn't come out yet. What are people doing for Communion? Where is King's in the whole transubstantiation debate? Is the wafer really Jesus, or a representation? I figure out that I'll just follow along with what everyone else does. I go in and there are benches sitting out the way they do in my time, too, in the back, away from the choir stalls. I spy Matthew sitting up in the front where the important leading scholars are, and I decide to follow along whatever he does. Or whatever the common people around me are doing, if he seems to be doing something odd.

But it really doesn't matter. The clergy don't expect the commoners to know what's going on, and so I just sit back and lose myself in the music. The prayer service is set by Tallis, and apparently the music has just arrived, a King's Premiere. The choir files in, and there are very few candles. It's dark and shadowy, and I'm lost in the liturgy and the harmonies. The English choral Renaissance reaches it's soaring heights under Elizabeth, but it's amazing to see its roots happening live, right in front of me. Talk about being part of history. Here I am in this amazing Chapel, just after it was completed, listening to music that has endured for 500 years, being premiered, live. For a few moments I forget how desperate I am to be home, and just soak in the experience.

I'm looking around so much, that I'm not conscious of the fact that my hood is slipping away from my face a bit. Not a lot, but more of my face is exposed than before. Then I feel someone looking at me, and I turn my head to see Edward staring right at me, his bony face in a permanent scowl. Oh crap. I should have been more careful. This isn't good. I feel a chill running down my spine, and inwardly curse myself for being so careless. I would love to leave, to just run out and swim back to our village. But that would be too obvious, and he might just have me arrested or something. No, I need to not draw any attention to myself, and just file out with the rest of the people after the service.

I spend the rest of the service worried about Edward seeing me, keeping my face covered, though I know it's too late to do anything, and I'm obsessed with watching him to see if he's making any sudden moves. Eventually the choir of boys and men files back down the aisle out of the Chapel, and it's safe to leave. I walk quickly, but not obviously escaping, back to the boat at the King's dock where Joseph is waiting for me. He helps me into the boat, still in my robe. I'm not taking the risk of going back to Matthew's rooms to return it to him. I feel a surge of relief as the boat pulls away and I know I'm headed back towards the safety of the island. But as I leave I turn around, and I see Edward, standing near the dock, staring out at us.

A feeling of iciness moves down my back again, and it's not just from the rain, which has resumed falling. We move away and I whisper a silent prayer for myself, Alice and Matthew.

I am beginning to think of Alice's little cottage as my own, and so I am filled with relief as we approach the little island and I see the glow of candlelight seeping out from under the door and shuttered windows. I know she's in there, staying up to talk to me, and for that I feel so incredibly grateful. Having me here has made life even more difficult for her. She has had to explain my presence to everyone who comes by (and with winter coming and colds starting up, there have been lots of people), worry about protecting me, and being discovered taking care of me. It can't have been easy for her.

I leave the waterman from King's and watch him headed back to the city. He has turned down my offer of a drink, wanting to get back, and I watch him disappear into the mist, and then turn into the cottage.

Alice greets me excitedly. I've been away for most of the day and she's been worried, so I fill her in on everything, telling her about my conversation with Sophie, and I even talk about the choral service at King's. She listens to everything, thrilled for me that getting home seems to be a lot more of a possibility than it was two days ago, but worried that Edward had seen me and I took such a risk just to hear choral music. Then her face blanches when I tell her how he watched us leaving.

"You took such a risk, Natasha. You are foolish, indeed. And now you have placed me in danger as well."

She's really angry and goes to bed without speaking to me. I lay on the furs with Paddy, feeling as if he is also holding a grudge, and try not to worry about everything that can go wrong now.

There's nothing I can do to change it. Edward is definitely a threat, and I need to be much more mindful moving forward.

CHAPTER SEVENTEEN

Implementation

The next day, midmorning, I get a text from Sophie. "Call me when you can." It's a rare sunny day, and I ask Alice if she thinks I might be able to charge my phone outside in the garden without people noticing. She says she thinks it's worth a try, and she can come out and feed the chickens and keep an eye out for me, and if needed, sit down next to me to hide the charger.

I call Sophie immediately.

"hey, whatcha doin?" she asks.

"Sitting in a chicken coop. Say hey to Alice."

Alice looks horrified.

"Hey Alice, thanks for taking care of my friend," Sophie says.

"You're welcome" Alice screams. She reminds me of my grandma trying to use a cell phone. I'm not sure if she thinks that Sophie could hear her better over 500 years if she yells more or what.

"So, I did a little bit of research on this Music of the Spheres thing."

"Ok, talk fast. I don't know how long my battery is going to last."

Sophie speeds up. "It was conceived by Pythagoras. He theorized that the planets in their orbits must make some kind of vibrations, and they would be perfect intervals or something. Ptolemy also talked about it. But really, it started getting wider appreciation during the Renaissanace when the work of a 5th century Roman Philosopher called Boethius was reprinted. He also believed in the music of the spheres, and he thought that each planet had its own harmony or something, and that you could cure people of their illnesses if you were able to play scales tuned to the music of a planet that was linked to the illness. Also, did you know that in the middle ages they had like 8 types of scales? They had all these kinds for each type of illness. There was a lot of debate over how you could hear the music of the spheres, and most people thought you had to be dead, or part of the spirit world or whatever to hear it. But if you accidentally heard something like the music of the spheres while you were still alive, it could kind of mess you up, too. And you know, even now NASA scientists have found that different particles emit vibrations, and they're able to translate those vibrations into music. And a physicist who studied string theory also wrote that they had vibrations and made noises, so it's not really as far fetched as it seems."

"Wow, Sophie, this is awesome information. How did you find it all?"

"Oh, there was an In Our Time episode on it a few years ago. Melvyn Bragg knows everything."

I'm sidetracked thinking about the intelligent host of my favorite radio program. "He really does, doesn't he?"

"So listen Tasha. I don't think that their theory about the music of the spheres somehow being linked to your time travel is really all that off base. It's possible that the planets were aligned in such a way at just the moment that you happened to hear some kind of chord that matched up with the alignment, and it was enough to send you off kilter for a second, and bring you back there."

"Well that's a great theory, but how do I get back?"

"I'm thinking that the best thing we could do is get an astronomer to put together some kind of chart of how the planets were aligned when you got stuck, and then also we could match it up to the chords in the music you were hearing. We'd need the exact longitude and latitude of where you were, I think, and a copy of the score so that we could see exactly what interval you heard. If we were able to recreate it at a time when the planets were in the same rotation or whatever, or even opposite maybe, then it might work in the opposite direction."

"Oh this is getting really complicated."

"Did you expect it to be simple?"

"I'm not sure. It seemed simple when it happened."

"You're stuck in time, Tasha. Of course it's not going to be simple to get you back. We need to recreate magic here. Honestly, you think we can just do that without any planning? Like lightening will just strike twice?"

"Well, it struck once. I thought maybe it would easily strike again?"

"I'm going to come up to Cambridge at the weekend. Simon knows a physicist at Sidney Sussex college. I'm going to speak with him. I also want to know exactly where you were in King's so we can get the right measurements."

"Sophie..."

"Yes?"

"Thank you."

"You're welcome. I'm not doing this just for you, though. I need a day out, and anyway, I miss you. Work isn't nearly as fun. Howard is on a rampage. I told him you were going into rehab."

"You what?"

"For sex addiction. In Los Angeles. That place in Malibu celebrities are always checking into."

"Promises?"

"That's the one. I told him you had checked yourself in there for sex addiction and alcoholism, and you couldn't be reached. You have no idea how pissed off he is."

"Oh shit. How will I ever make things right?"

"Tasha this ship has sailed. Even if you make it back to this century, you won't be working for Howard again, I can guarantee it."

"It's for the best anyway, I guess. That job was really stressing me out and probably contributing to whatever addictions I may or may not have."

"Exactly. I'm thinking you will go out on your own or something."

"Hey Soph? Can you check on my cat?"

"Already done. Mrs. Wiggles is doing just fine and is staying with us."

"Oh, you are a star."

"It's nothing. The kids like having another playmate. So when I come up on Saturday I'm going to call you. Do you think you can be available to talk with this guy?"

"Sure, maybe I'll see if I can go to Matthew's and maybe Richard can come back, too."

"Fine. Oh, and one more thing."

"Yep?"

"it's not good news. I went to the British Library this morning and did some searching around in the records of the scholars and monks at King's, and there was an Edward. I saw Matthew listed, too, but he disappeared suddenly from the records. Everyone thinks he was probably killed secretively for being a reformer a little too early or someone had an agenda against him. Edward continued to rise, and under Mary Tudor he actually was a leader in persecuting many of the Protestants that she burned as heretics. He was in league with Mary's advisors Gardiner and Pole. You need to be careful with him and watch your back."

I look at Alice who looks back at me with large fearful eyes.

"Doesn't surprise me, and sadly, I'm already failing."

I tell her about what happened the night before, and hearing it again, Alice looks like she might breathe fire. They both are angry with me. Sophie for being stupid, and Alice for being stupid while I'm staying with her, which is inadvertently making her stupid, too. Point taken. I'm going to be more careful.

Sophie signs off because she has a lunch appointment, and Alice and I sit in the dirt with the chickens in silence.

"He's evil, Edward."

"I think you're right."

"He lusts for blood."

"Alice," an idea is starting to form in my head. "If I can figure out how to get back, why don't you come with me? You would be safe in my century. You could train as a doctor, or a nurse. You could use your knowledge and help people. Maybe we could persuade Matthew to come along too, and you two could actually get married or stop giving each other sideways glances thinking you're being secretive when really you're just being really obvious."

She blushes a little bit at that.

"Are Matthew and I that transparent?"

"You are. He's the father, right? Of Rose?

"He was. Yes."

"And everyone here knows about it and that's why you're so protected in this village, right?"

"Also correct."

"You should come with me."

"But Natasha, you know yourself how hard it is being apart from where you belong. I don't know if I could do it."

"The thing is, Alice, I don't know that you actually belong here. I know I belong back home. I know for a fact that I do not belong here. But I'm starting to suspect that you don't belong here either."

"I'll think about it. And anyway, who knows if you'll even be able to get back."

I sigh. Obviously I've thought about it. But I hate the idea.

"If you can't, then what would you do?"

"I really don't know, Alice. I suppose I could go to London and maybe get in on the book printing business? The thing is, I know a lot about what's going to happen over the next few decades here. I could start to print William Shakespeare's books before anyone else would.

That's it! I could be a literary agent, based in Stratford."

She looks at me with a curious expression.

"He was a super famous writer who will start to take off in a few decades," I tell her.

"In the immediate future, my plan is to not get myself killed. If I do wind up here for a while longer, things are going to get very muddled and I don't want to be anywhere near it. So I'd like to lie low. Maybe run away somewhere. To Ireland or something."

"What's going to happen to England, Natasha?"

"Will you promise to use the knowledge I'm about to tell you for you only? Not to tell others? And to use it for your protection?"

"I will.

"Swear it."

"I give you my oath."

"Ok. Henry is going to marry six times, as I told Matthew before."

"Heavens!"

"And when he dies, his son Edward is going to be the king, but he'll still be a young boy. He will be under the guidance of Protestants and others who have an agenda in favor of the new religion. Masses will be outlawed. But then Edward is going to die young. Still a teenager. Mary Tudor will take his place. And she, of course, is still ardently Catholic and decides to mend the breach with Rome. She puts England back under papal jurisdiction and starts to burn heretics. Cranmer is killed. There's a whole book of protestants who were martyred under Mary. They call her Bloody Mary. But then she dies after only five years, and has no children. Elizabeth takes the throne. And Alice, she is a good queen. She rules for 45 years. She is largely protestant, but doesn't really burn heretics except some Jesuit priests she thinks are a threat to her rule. She puts on armor and leads an army to defeat the Spanish Armada. It is a good time to be English under her. She never marries, and is called the Virgin Queen. After her, the Stuart line takes the throne."

"So things will be difficult for the next 20-odd years, and then it will be good?"

"I suppose so, yes."

"But Natasha..."

"Mmm?"

"We probably won't be alive in 20 years to appreciate it."

"What do you mean? I'll only be like 55."

"That is ancient."

"Oh. Right. Oh Alice, this sucks. In my century there's medicine. Simple things like antibiotics that kill bacteria. Vaccines against measles and chicken pox. People live until they're 80 and 100 regularly."

"It sounds like a time filled with miracles."

"It is! It really is! You should come back Alice. You can train and be a midwife. You could open your own practice. It would be amazing."

Alice's eyes are shining and she looks excited. "I promise you I will think about it."

And that's good enough for me for now.

We sit amiably outside in the rare sunshine while my phone charges, the chickens prance and cluck around, and I check Facebook. All my friends wonder where I am, which is heartening, I guess. Only I don't know what to tell them, so I just flick away to Amazon where I download more and more books. If I am stuck here for a while, I want to have a good supply of reading material.

The more my mind turns it over, the more I really want Alice and Matthew both to come with me. Matthew's mind and curiosity need to be where he can explore and have access to Google. He needs to be let loose in the British Library. Or the Smithsonian archives or something. And they could be together. Of course, there's the odd question of how they would get National Health card, ID cards, and everything like that. But it's percolating in my head, and I want to continue to think about it.

For now, my next appointment looms. A physicist in Cambridge is meeting with Sophie on Saturday at noon. I'd really like to be around. I know it's not like I'll be able to see her, but knowing that I'm standing nearby would be comforting. I send Matthew a message to see whether it would be ok if I come for a visit then, and he responds that he would love to have me, and would love to hear the physicist speak as well. He doesn't even know what a physicist is, but he's excited by it.

On Friday it's sunny, but it feels as if rain might be coming. It's odd how I can start to feel it now. I used to just rely on Weather Underground, but now my bones are starting to be able to feel the weather. I am feeling more attuned to nature and to the ground, the earth, the elements than I ever have before. More like I'm part of nature and the life cycle, and not just a consumer of it. I've been here nearly a month, and I'm already starting to feel different. The homespun cloth doesn't seem to itch as much. Or maybe it's just that I'm super filthy and the layer of dirt protects me. But I can start to see how people make lives here, and for the most part, the simplicity is appealing. Don't get me wrong, I still want to get back. I would literally kill for some fries from McDonald's right now. But I am feeling deeply contented in a way I never have before.

I need to figure out how I can bring more of this feeling back home with me. I know, for example, that not drinking alcohol and spending quiet time in contemplation and meditation regularly will help. I suppose doing more to bring me close to nature, like gardening, cooking with good foods rather than throwing things in the microwave, making more from scratch in general. I wonder whether I will become all crafty and post pictures of my creations on pinterest. The idea of me turning from serious career woman to homemade etsy-selling gardener makes me laugh.

Since it feels like rain is coming, I decide to charge my phone so I have enough juice to see me through a phone call with Sophie. I sit out in the chicken yard, which gets the most sunlight, and Paddy joins me. I am playing around looking at TMZ when someone comes for Alice, but she's not home. She's run over to the home of her friend Susan who is having a rough pregnancy, and needed some help. So I don't hear the footsteps until it's too late and a man I've never seen before, who looks very unhappy, pops his head around before I can hide my phone. I frantically move my cloak to cover it, but a part of the solar charger is still sticking out, and I'm sure he can see it. He doesn't say anything, though.

"What are you doing sitting out here," he asks, looking at me curiously.

"Just, you know, enjoying the sun. We won't get it for a while again, it feels like."

"You're staying with Alice, right."

"Yes. She's gone over to Susan's house, she said."

"Please tell her that John Mason was here."

"Absolutely, I will. Does she know where you live, Mr. Mason?"

"She does. You're not from here, are you?"

"Oh, no, I grew up in the West Country. Around Glastonbury. I was in London with my husband when he died. Alice and I are cousins, and so I came up here with a group of pilgrims who were traveling to Ely. Just until I figure out whether to go back home and what to do."

I'm committing the number one mistake of people who have something to hide. I'm talking way too much and answering questions that no one has asked. The more I talk, the more John Mason stares at me.

"Well, just tell her I came, will you?"

"Should I tell her what it's about?"

"She'll know."

That sounds ominous.

"All right. Peace be with you, Mr. Mason."

I think that sounds pious, but again he looks at me funny. I'm just fucking this up right and left, and he does not look like a man that it's a good idea to fuck up around.

When he leaves I dig my phone back out, and Facebook message Sophie, confirming what time she's coming up tomorrow, and tell her what happened with John Mason. She starts panicking on my behalf, and decides to Google him as well. She messages back after a few minutes.

"Oh Sophie, you pick the worst people. I think he worked with your Edward character to persecute protestants under Mary. We really need to get you out of there."

When Alice comes home I told her what happened, and she takes a deep breath. "I owe him some money. It's ok. He won't hurt you."

Things in this little village are starting to seem quite scary, and instead of feeling like a refuge, it's feeling a bit like a prison.

CHAPTER EIGHTEEN

Trouble Starts Brewing

The next day at about 11am I am outside waiting for the waterman. It's Joseph, and I know him already because he took me the last time. Matthew says he's trustworthy, but now I'm starting to panic so much about everyone, I don't know who I can turn to. So I keep my phone hidden again, and avoid conversation as we slide through the water.

Joseph doesn't say much to me. He seems to sense that I want to be left alone. But towards the end, as we're punting down the Cam past the backs of the colleges, he turns around.

"Madame Margaret," he starts. For a second I don't know who he's talking to, but then I remember that's my name here.

"Yes?"

"You should know, ma'am, that people are starting to talk about you. Saying you're not who you say you are. Saying even that you have brought Devices of the Devil to our town."

"Who is saying this, Joseph?"

"I think you know. Your suspicions are correct. Watch yourself. That's all I'm saying."

I take a deep breath. I seriously hate being a woman in the 16th century. "Thank you, Joseph. I appreciate your honesty with me."

"I like you all right, and Matthew has been good to me. If he trusts you, then I do too."

"Again, you have my thanks. Sadly, I do not have any money, so my thanks and appreciation will have to do."

He smiles at me. "It's ok. Matthew pays me well to come out to your village. He sends me to Alice, too."

Of course. Joseph must be some kind of messenger.

I really need to talk to Matthew about all of these things that are happening, but it's nearly noon, and I need to take the call from Sophie. Unfortunately I don't see Matthew anywhere, and he normally greets me here to escort me to his room. I don't want to just take the call out in public. As if I'm not suspicious enough anyway, the idea of me talking to myself into a little black device in front of everyone would really be odd.

Suddenly I am feeling so claustrophobic, and I know I need to get out of this city, this time period, and get home. I still have my cloak from the other night, which I am wrapped in, and so I pull the hood up and head towards the Chapel from the river. With the hood pulled up over my face, I am inconspicuous, and I pass into the Chapel unquestioned.

I don't see Matthew anywhere, and according to the clock on my phone I still have about 15 minutes, so I decide to go into the Chapel itself, which looks so similar to how I know it, it freaks me out a bit. I kneel down and close my eyes and pretend to pray, when some of the brothers walk past me going to their noon service. I spy brother Edward, who looks very severe as usual, and I hear the words, "under his leadership, Cambridge is becoming a bastion of heretical thought, just like Oxford. And all these strangers he keeps bringing in. It's just not Godly."

They must be talking about Matthew. Things seem to be turning downwards for him, and since I'm linked to him, if things get bad for him, they will get bad for me. And Alice.

"But what can we do with all of the changes the privy council keeps introducing?" one of the other brothers responds. "It's not all down to him. He can't fight Cromwell."

I try to think about the timeline what's happening now. It's the end of November, 1539. Anne of Cleves is most likely on her way over to England from Germany, to be Henry's fourth wife. He will find her so unattractive that he will claim he couldn't consummate the marriage, and has it annulled by July. Cromwell, who negotiated the treaty, is starting to overreach his powers and his list of enemies is growing; in less than a year he'll be dead, taking the fall for the King's dislike of his new wife.

I hide my face and walk back to Matthew's rooms and listen through the thick door. I don't hear sounds. I knock, not sure what I'll do if someone other than Matthew answers. I keep my face hidden under the hood, and turned away, in case it's not him, but fortunately for me it is. Unfortunately for me, and him, he has clearly been in a pretty serious fight, and is bleeding and groaning.

He collapses back in his chair, and I run over, and try to help him. I ask him what happened, and he moans. I wish I had some ice for his bleeding, but I don't, so I fish around in my bag for a nurofen, and give it to him. "Here, this will help. I promise." He takes it, and I wrap some cloth around his cuts, and then look at the clock on my phone.

I can't spend any more time dealing with this right now, but I need to take the call from Sophie that is coming in.

--

"Natasha, excellent, I'm so glad you picked up. I have Julian Breen here with me. I've briefed him on what happened to you, so he's up to speed as much as I am."

"Great, well, things just took on a new level of intensity here now, guys."

"Hello Natasha, Julian here, so great to speak with you finally. This is so exciting."

"Yeah, well, my protector has just had the shit beaten out of him."

"Wait, Natasha, what are you talking about?"

"I'm in Matthew's rooms. He didn't answer at first. I came in, and dude is on the ground, bleeding like crazy."

"Oh shit. Edward?" Sophie asks.

"I really don't know. I haven't spoken with him yet. I'm sitting in his chair talking to you, but I'm talking really quietly in case anyone walks past. I'm trying to stop the bleeding coming from the cut in his face, so forgive me for being a tad bit distracted."

"Ok, listen, we'll talk fast. Julian and I are in the King's College Chapel."

"So close and yet so far..."

"I know sweetie. We're doing what we can. We are standing near the choir. Where were you exactly? Julian wants to figure out longitude and latitude."

"I was in one of the chairs closest to the painting. Maybe three or four rows back from it? And I was in the front of the aisle. Left side as you're looking at the painting."

"Natasha, Julian here," his voice cuts in, confident and self assured. Even with all that is happening with Matthew now, I have a good feeling about this fellow. Sophie found someone smart, I can tell.

"I was looking at the way the different stars were aligned on November 1, and checking to see if there were any unusual sorts of patterns or something I could detect, and it does appear that there were a larger amount of sunspots than normal, and the storm in Jupiter's eye seemed to get stronger. It was also a full moon. That leads me to believe that there may have been some vibration patterns moving through space that happened to intersect where you were, especially depending on what chord you were listening to at the time. The medieval idea of the Music of the Spheres isn't that off base, to be honest."

He takes a breath, and continues.

"Now, the conditions haven't really changed and it appears that the solar storm will be going on for at least another few weeks, but if that's the case, then the trick is going to be to get you in the exact same spot, listening to the same music in the same type of setting so that the vibrations can all match up like before. And on a full moon, which is in a week. Do you think you could arrange to have the choir there learn the O Magnum Mysterium, and you could have it performed at a 3:30pm Evensong, and sit exactly where you were? Also, you'd need to make sure the tempo was the same, and that you started at exactly the same time."

You are kidding me, I think.

"You are kidding me," I say.

"Tasha, you are stuck in time. We're offering you a way that you might be able to get back," Sophie jumps in.

"Yeah, and how am I supposed to get the choir to perform this at that exact time? Especially when the guy who I thought was the head guy, who could have maybe helped me, is lying in his bed right now, wrecked."

Sophie ignores my protests, and she's right to do so. After all, it's not like I have a lot of options right now. "I'm going to send you a copy of the music to your email. Can you get email? It's in a pdf. I can't mail it obviously. But you should be able to work with the choir so they can learn their parts."

"Yes, make sure it's you working with them, Natasha" pipes in Julian, ever so helpfully. "We need to make sure you have the sound right. People in the 16th century didn't understand musical notation the way we do."

"I'm emailing it to you now - can you confirm that you got it?" Sophie is businesslike as ever.

I hear the beep and see the comforting gmail envelope on my screen. "Got it. Thank you. Let me get Matthew fixed up here, and see what I can do. God, I wish you could just come over here and help me. I'm not even like 200 feet from you."

"I'm coming over. Which rooms are you in?"

"The very back. He's the boss. The big ones."

Sophie starts walking - I hear her footsteps through the phone, and then I hear her again.

"I'm standing in the doorway. It was open. Where are you now?"

"Do you see the fireplace to your right? Is it still there?"

"Yes."

"I'm all the way on the far side. Between the fireplace and the window. Oh God, Sophie, I miss you so much. I miss everyone so much. I really really really want to come home."

She's silent and I swear that for a moment I can feel her hugging me.

"Natasha, you are tough. You got to England on your own. You basically run a giant publishing company. You can do this. You can figure this out. Next full moon. You make this happen too, ok? I know you can do this. You have a week to get it together. I know you can. I'm hugging you now."

I start sobbing into the phone, utterly confused by the scene in front of me, and how I can ever square off the circle so that it makes sense again.

"Don't get all soft on me now. I need you to be strong. You need you to be strong."

"Sophie. I have one more favor."

"Yes?"

"Could you look into how to get two fake id's. One for a woman, about 25. One for a man, about 28."

"Matthew and Alice?"

"Yes, I want to bring them with me."

"Can you imagine how hard that will be for them?"

"Obviously, I can. But they are in danger here, and I think that would be worse than adjusting to a new life in the future."

"Well, I'll check into it. I know a guy."

"You always know a guy. A Cambridge Physicist. A guy for fake ID's. You know everyone. Thank you Sophie."

"it's ok. I just want you back. We'll figure this out."

We hang up the phone, with me keenly aware that I don't deserve a friend like her, and Matthew starts groaning. I go over to him and kneel down beside him. "Matthew, you have to tell me what happened."

"Edward. Cromwell. It's all...related," he whispers.

"What's all related, what does this mean?"

Matthew just motions that he wants to be propped up, and I help him. He's leaning on me, and I realize that I barely even notice how much he smells. Goodness, I must really be getting used to the 16th century.

He lays down, and I want to go fetch some water for him, but he just points to the mead. I pour some for him, and he drinks it slowly, taking long sips with pauses in between. Then he looks up at me with his eyes big, and full of fear. He takes some deep breaths, and then starts to talk, very slowly at first.

"You were right about Cromwell's fall. It's beginning. Gardiner's star is on the rise, and he is Cromwell's sworn enemy. I am Cromwell's man. Edward is Gardiner's. They know about

Alice. They suspect me of heresy. They suspect you. The penalty for heresy is to be burned alive. Oh Natasha, it's all falling apart."

"And did Gardiner send some thugs here to warn you? To send a message that your time of comfort was coming to an end?"

"I believe so, yes. They just came in and surprised me, and called me some names, and told me that I needed to stop supporting the Devil."

"Your waterman mentioned something as well."

"Joseph? He's not in with them, surely."

"Matthew, I don't really know who I can trust anymore. And yesterday a strange man showed up at the house saying Alice owed him money. She seemed to know who he was."

"Oh, Sophie, it's all unravelling around us. I had worked for reform, but reform that wouldn't hurt anyone. I don't want the holy houses to be destroyed. Only the corrupt ones. I want people to have access to the holy Word of God. I want people to be educated, and seek a relationship with the Lord!"

Matthew is heating up now, the passion he feels must outweigh the pain in his ribs.

"Matthew, did you hear any of my conversation I just had?"

"Not really. Bits."

"That was my friend Sophie. She's in Cambridge now with a very intelligent physicist. He had done a bit of research looking at the way the planets were aligned and he has a theory that the Morten Lauridsen piece somehow had a vibration that was exactly in tune with some solar flares and something about Jupiter's spot, and who knows what else, probably something with string theory in there as well, but anyway, the point is, he believes that if we act fast to recreate the situation I was in, I can get back."

He momentarily loses the anguish in his eyes and looks happy. "Oh, that's wonderful news, Sophie."

"And you and Alice could come with me."

"Sophie, I don't know.... I couldn't leave...there is so much work to be done here..."

"Matthew, how? Cromwell is falling. You were his man, right? Things are going to be good for a while for you under Edward, but then they get very bad very quickly under Mary, if you even survive till then. And you could be together with Alice in our time. I held on to my bag last time, and everything that was in it came with me. I think that if we're all touching, you could come along, too."

"I can't decide that right now. Have you even asked Alice about her thoughts on this?"

"I brought it up, perhaps. I think it makes the most sense. She could train as a midwife or nurse. She could actually really help people and use her knowledge to make such a difference without being suspected of being a witch because she can heal people. And she could be with you. And she could be exploring her own intellect. What is there to lose?"

"Sophie, I need some time to consider. It's an appealing idea. I love the society that you discuss living in. I find it fascinating, and I would love to experience it. But to just leave?"

"What do you have keeping you here?"

"I need to rest, Sophie. Let's concentrate on making it possible for you to go back, which, if things keep going as they are trending is going to be more and more difficult. What do you need?"

"Not much. Just your choir for some rehearsals, and the Chapel with the choir for a 3:30pm Evensong service the next full moon."

"which is when?"

"Next Saturday; a week from today."

"Ok, I can't guarantee anything. Who knows if I'll even be well enough to make requests or push people around. But we'll try our best."

Up until now it hasn't even occurred to me that Richard Chancellor hasn't shown up for this meeting. I suspect he was sidetracked in London. But it's a shame that he wasn't here to take care of Matthew, and perhaps could have stopped this from happening to him. When I bring it up, Matthew just nods, and looks worried.

"I hope he isn't mixed up in this at all. He's the only other person who knows about you who could attract attention, and I wouldn't want him giving anything away."

CHAPTER NINETEEN

Another Sunday

I leave Matthew a few of my nurofen tablets for him to take later, and walk back through the dreary fog to Joseph the waterman. I'm feeling a little more suspicious of him, and the ride back to the island village seems just slightly more sinister. I'm glad to be going back before dark, though. There is still some other traffic on the river, and I don't feel as alone or frightened as I would if it was dark and we were the only boat on the water. He doesn't say anything to me again, and I'm not sure whether I should thank him for warning me before, or if I should be wary of him. Either way, I'm not doing any talking.

When we get back home, and I'm safely in the comfort of the thatched roof cottage, with Paddy purring on me to welcome me back, Alice gets a full rundown of the day, including what happened to Matthew. She is quiet, and looks at her hands, not showing emotion. Of course she is. What can she say?

"Alice, I am worried that the man who came to see you yesterday is linked to this somehow. I am worried that things are going to get very bad for you, very quickly. I don't know enough about your life to know what you will do without Matthew, but I don't think you can count on him for a very long time. It appears that his star is in the descent, and the wheel of fortune is not favoring him right now. I am going to do everything I can to get back to my time, because frankly, I am scared, and I want to go home. I'm going to try to become a choir director and teach this music to the choir. And I'm going to figure out how to get an Evensong service done in King's next week when there will be a full moon. But Alice, I'm worried about leaving you. I can't help you here. I'm lost here. I don't even know how to go through the motions of a church service. But I can help you in my time, if you'll let me. Please consider coming back with me, if it works. I can't even guarantee that it will work, but please say that you'll consider coming back if it does. I can't think of any other way I can repay you other than by taking good care of you, and I can only do that in my time."

"I understand your words, Natasha. I really do. And I appreciate you looking out for me. But I feel that if it's fate that something happen to me, then it's fate, and how can I argue that?"

"You can argue it by changing fate. Maybe it's fate that I was supposed to come here and talk to you and bring you back. Maybe that's your fate. Why does living a miserable life have to be fate?"

"Everything I know is here."

"You can get to know new things. Alice, I'm not saying this lightly. I know how hard it would be for you. Of course I do. I'm living it right now. But I also know that right now is a dangerous time for you, and in my time things could be more secure. I also know that there is very little holding you back, and if Matthew came along too, then things could be so different for you both."

She looks up suddenly at that. "Is Matthew going to go? Have you spoken with him?"

"He wasn't in any state to talk, but he said he'd think about it."

"Well, I will think about it as well. Everything you say is true, of course. But it's equally true that I love my home, and even though I shouldn't according to you, I do feel safe here."

"Ok, suit yourself. I've got some music to learn. I'm going to try to go into King's tomorrow to see if I can figure out how to get the choir. We've only got a week. I need them to rehearse with me."

"You are taking some risks."

"I have to if I want to get back."

In the middle of the night I wake up cold - the fire is dying, and Paddy has left me. My blankets are cold and the wind has picked up outside. This never ending wind coming in off the North Sea, whipping across the swampland.

I reluctantly get out of my blankets to go put another log on the fire and try to get it going again, when I hear sobs coming from the bed next to the kitchen area. Alice is crying, and it appears that Paddy has deserted me in order to comfort his mistress, which I find sweet.

I put the log on the embers, and once the flames start to pick up, I walk over and get into her bed with her.

"Alice, what's the matter?"

"I'm scared. If I stay here, I could be killed as a witch. My animals could be killed. Everything I love could be taken from me. But if I go, I lose my friends, and I still lose my animals. I don't know what the point would be of even being alive if I can't be with the people and animals I love."

I wrap my arms around her, both to calm her, and to warm up. And we lay there in silence, spooning with the cats, and her crying into her furs. And I wonder...

"Alice. Do your animals travel well?"

"What does that mean?"

"I mean, could you put them in a big bag that you could hold on to, at the very end? Everything in my purse came with me.

What if we bundled you up in a big cloak, and you had the bag underneath you. Do you think you could carry them all?"

"I could try. It would be better than losing them. Though, do you think they could make the journey?"

"I don't know why they couldn't. If my iphone made it intact, surely grumpy old Paddy can, with just a bit of grumbling on his part."

"I'll think more carefully about it. If you think he can make it."

I don't get out of bed, but Alice stops crying and we both drift back to sleep.

I wake up in the morning and go off to Church again with Alice, for the fourth Sunday, and I seem to be fitting in. This has been the most interaction I get with the townspeople, and most of them seem to be starting to feel friendly to me. The advent season is beginning, and I am heartened by recognizing some of the hymns I still sing, like O Come O Come Emmanual. Standing there in the darkness (for it barely gets light by 9am now, and I'm not sure that you could even call it light when the sun finally comes up. The Log Angeles girl in me is sorely missing the vitamin D) and watching the candles flicker with the wreaths and holly leaves being put up throughout the Chapel makes me feel at home, and at peace, for once. Also, the fact that I may wind up being able to get back home in the next week, and might never be in this damp swampy church again in my life might be the more comforting factor. It really is frighteningly cold here. Which kind of tells me something about the disposition of the Vikings, if they found this preferable to their own country.

As we're singing these advent hymns, it dawns on me how I can get the Chapel of King's on Saturday at 3:30pm, a time that isn't normally set aside for services, especially services that don't exist yet. What about a special Advent music service? We don't have to call it an Evensong service. We can just call it a Christmas Advent service. That way the church shouldn't be too angry at Matthew for holding a service that doesn't fit in with the current liturgy. I smile at this simple and elegant solution, and I think that Matthew should be pleased with me for thinking of it.

I want to go and see him, but I don't trust his waterman Joseph anymore. After service as Alice is greeting her friends, a large family comes over to say hello. Surprisingly I haven't yet met everyone on the island. I suppose it's all my journeys to Cambridge, and hiding in the house so as to not say anything to give myself away. I recognize a heavily pregnant woman from my first Sunday here when she came to Alice's house with concerns over her baby not moving. She now has four other children of various ages attached to her, or following behind. I remember that Alice was called away the other day to her friend's house who was having a difficult pregnancy, and suspect it is the same woman. She looks like she could pop at any moment.

"Hello my love," she comes over to hug Alice, who hugs her back, squishing between them the toddler in her arms, who looks delighted at the displays of affection. "I don't know what I'd have done without you. The contractions are starting to be close and painful."

"That's a sign that it's going to come soon," Alice says, to the woman's obvious delight, but her husband doesn't react at all, just staring straight ahead, ignoring the little boy who is jumping up and down next to him. He must be feeling overwhelmed, I think.

"Susan, this is Margaret," she says, introducing me in my different more timely name.

"Margaret has been staying with me. She's a distant cousin, but from the West Country. I told you about her the other day.

Margaret, Susan is one of my dearest friends, and also obviously about to have a child."

"I've heard about you," Susan says, with a wink in her eye. "You've been a bit out of place, haven't you?"

I'm not exactly sure what that means, but decide that I need to stop seeing a sinister motive in everything, so I just answer with a simple, "yes, things are quite different here than in Glastonbury."

"I hear there are monsters in the sea there," she asks, quite curiously.

"Yes, but they say that about here, so I suppose it's all in the eye of the beholder." And she laughs at that.

"Indeed. Alice, honestly, these pains. They are really starting to hurt. This is so much worse than with the others." She moves her hands over her protruding belly. I remember that noble women generally go into confinement six weeks before they are due. I suppose there is no such luxury for common women who need to work, not to mention the other children running around.

"Do you not have any kind of confinement period?" I ask innocently.

She stares at me in astonishment. "Do common women have confinements in Glastonbury? It must be an enormously wealthy place."

"Oh, well, only as they get very close to their time," I answer, making it up on the fly.

"Not so here," she says. "I only wish, given how hard this is. All I want is to lie down with my feet up, but even that hurts! My back is killing me. At least today I can rest, as long as this one naps!" she says, cooing over the toddler.

All the pregnancy talk is making the husband uncomfortable, and he goes off to another group of men to talk about sports or something (what do men talk about after church here?) while we continue walking along back to Susan's house.

"There's so much to be done before the baby comes," Susan continues. "The sheep are mostly taken care of for the winter, but there is still so much left undone. At least the older children can help now."

"There is never a right time to have a baby, and whatever time you will have the baby is the perfect time. It's one of the great mysteries of life," Alice imparts her wisdom, and takes the baby from Susan's arms. "You don't need to carry her this late in your time," she says.

"Harold was going into Cambridge today," Susan says, changing the subject. "He was meeting someone to talk about the sheep for the Spring. I know we aren't meant to be doing work on a Sunday," she looks at me as if she's afraid that I might report her. "But really, we don't have many other options right now. He's only in town for a few days. Anyway, if either of you need anything, he might be able to get it."

"Actually, how is he getting there?" I pipe in. Alice looks at me wonderingly. "Only, do you think he could take me along? I really need to speak with someone there myself. What if you went too, Alice? We could do something daring like visit a tavern."

"This crazy West Country girl," Alice looks at me, as if that explains it all.

"I think he should be able to take the two of you, though I hate to be left alone here. What if I go into labor for real?"

Alice feels her belly, pushes a few places, rests her ear on it, feels around a little more, and then proclaims, "I don't think you will for another few days. The contractions right now are your body's way of practicing. Every pregnancy is different, and this baby wants to do it perfectly, so is just practicing a bit more."

"How can you know that?" Susan demands.

"The baby told me," she responds.

"Well did it tell you if it's a boy or a girl, because I would love to start thinking about names!"

"Some things it keeps silent, even to me," Alice responds gravely.

Back at Susan's, I look around her cottage, which is similar to Alice's in size, but has a bit more stuff. Not a lot, considering there are four - almost five - children. A large bed which they must all share, along with a very few wooden toys are the only evidence that there are children living there. The older children run around outside playing a form of tag, while the young ones cling to their mother's skirts. We prepare a lunch of a fresh chicken who was just killed this morning, along with some onions, carrots, and celery. All the best root vegetables, I think.

"Pretty soon I won't be able to cook like this again for a while," Susan jokes to Harold when he comes back in. "My mother doesn't cook nearly so well."

"Is she staying with you after you have the baby?" I ask.

"Yes, she will come from Baldock as soon as the baby starts to officially come, and she'll stay for as long as we need her. It'll be good to have her helping with the others."

"Hopefully not too long!" Harold jokes. Mother in law issues, even five hundred years ago. Some things never change.

"By the way, you're taking Alice and Margaret here along with you to Cambridge if that's ok," Alice tells Harold. "I volunteered you. Margaret needs to speak to someone at one of the colleges."

"How do you know people at the colleges?" Harold asks, though with simple curiosity, not any kind of meanness. "It's a friend of a friend," I respond honestly. "I just need to check in with him about a plan I have and make sure it's ok."

"Oooh, planning and scheming here in our little village! Well, I never!" Alice laughs at the intrigue, which is normally something more associated with London.

"Sure, I'll take you. Can you meet me at the dock a bit after our dinner?" We both nod.

Back home at our cottage, Alice lays into me. "what are you thinking, going to see Matthew without his asking you! What do you think you're going to do, just show up and they'll let you in?"

"Alice, I have this cloak, remember?" I ask, holding up the cloak that Matthew gave me.

"People will think I'm from the college or at least local. I can go in and check on him, and see how he's healing, and also tell him the idea I have for how we can have an Evensong service on Saturday. You're coming with me, because you're going to talk with him about the potential of coming along back with me. And we're going to try to find a big enough bag for all the animals."

"Natasha, it really is kind of you, but this is so difficult for me," Alice begins. "I can't think of it now."

"You have a week to make up your mind, but at least you can start talking to him about it now," I respond.

CHAPTER TWENTY

Lunch Out

The sun has finally come out, and the journey along the water is pleasant enough. We make small talk with Harold about the baby. He doesn't seem as excited as I would expect, but I suppose after four it gets a bit old. I think of the high pregnancy loss rates, and infant mortality, and suspect that he's been through this more than four times. He's wondrously noncommittal about anything we ask him, but I suppose it's different for fathers here. Childbirth and rearing young children is firmly in the domain of women, and fathers aren't as involved as they are in modern times.

He drops us off at the public docks by Jesus Green and again we are walking down King's Parade through mud and excrement, past Trinity, which, despite the nasty weather has still had a great deal more work done to it, and on to King's, where I wrap up in my cloak and start to sneak down an alleyway to the back entrance of the Chapel. I tell Alice to stay out in the market area, and that Matthew and I will come and get her. She doesn't have a cloak on like mine, and I'm worried that she'll attract attention.

I rush through the side entrance over to the rooms on the courtyard side, and then cover my face and wander down to Matthew's rooms, passing some scholars and monks. I knock on his doors, and when he answers I'm pleased. He looks so much better than the day before. He seems rested, and as if he's healing.

"Matthew, I've got Alice with me - she's out in the market square. I've got an idea about how to set up a service on Saturday. And also, I think you both should come with me," I spit out all my words at once, and then pause for a breath.

"One thing at a time!" He hands me his long cloak to take out to her, still resting and not wanting to make the journey himself.

Five minutes later I'm handing it to Alice, and pulling her back into the Chapel through the side entrance in the alleyway that leads to the river, though she is reluctant and even afraid to go so deep into King's. We keep our heads down and look very scholarly and serious as we walk down to Matthew's room, and then knock and enter without waiting for him to open the door.

Alice rushes over to Matthew, seeing his injuries for the first time, and starts to check his bandages, going into caregiver mode. She makes sure he has mead to drink, and when she asks him what his pain is like he laughs that it's not very bad thanks to the nurofen I gave him yesterday.

I cough to bring the attention back to the service, and my plans.

"You should say that as a service to the community, and to bring the word of the Lord to people during these turbulent times, you're going to have an Advent service. It would explain why we would do an O Magnum Mysterium, and also why it would be at a special time."

"But I would need permission from the Bishop to do something like that."

"So write a letter asking for it. It won't get to him in time, and even if it does, you won't get a response. You can say that you wrote, and because you had received no response, you thought it was fine. And anyway, given the fact that you're both going to come back with me, I'm not really sure why it matters. We only need to get the choir ready and have things open up on Saturday.

How much say do you have over when the choir rehearses, and what they rehearse?"

Matthew shakes his head. "Please don't start asking me to come back again. Is that why you've brought Alice with you?" They look at each other uneasily.

"You can continue to think about it. It's fine. Take your time. But seriously, can you set up the choir rehearsals for me?"

"I will do what I can," Matthew promises.

I realize that's as much as I'm going to get from Matthew right now, and decide to make an exit so that he and Alice can be together for a little while before we have to go. Maybe they can talk each other into coming back with me.

I leave his room saying I'm going to go for a little walk around town, and while Alice looks a bit surprised, Matthew says he'd like for her to stay just a bit. As I close the door behind me, I see their heads pressed together in the deep conversation of a couple who has a shared history, and knows the other better than anyone else in the world.

I'd like to give them a good hour or so alone, so I decide to walk into town and see if I can find somewhere warm to spend the time. The idea of finding an old inn or pub is appealing. Restaurants like I know wouldn't exist, but surely there is a place serving food and drink to travelers and scholars? I assume so.

I am wandering along King's Parade, and I spy just the place - a tavern on the side of the road called the White Horse, and I see men going in so I assume it must be open. For a moment I am stopped because I remember that I don't have any money, but I reach down in my pockets thinking there may be a coin or two in the robes Matthew gave me. At home I'm always finding money I forgot I had in the pockets of my clothes after they go through the laundry. I'm hoping the same principle holds true here.

I reach around the inside of the cloak where the pockets are hiding, and my fingers wrap around something metal. When I pull it out, I am in luck! It's a golden coin, and I'm not sure of its value, but I assume that it must be enough for a glass of ale and a meat pie of some sort. I haven't had any restaurant food since I've been here. I'm not expecting The Ivy, but it will be nice to have a nice meal prepared for me and not feel guilty because I'm just taking up space in Alice's house.

When I go in through the thick doorway, I see that I'm not the only one who had this idea. The room is spacious. Whitewashed walls with timber beams, just the way you'd imagine a medieval tavern. And there are groups of what appear to be students all around, sitting on wooden stools around rough wooden tables talking heatedly. Everyone looks up at me when I enter, but seeing my robes from King's, they don't register that I am a woman, and go right back to their conversations.

I walk up to the counter where an older plump woman in filthy clothes asks me what my business is, looking at me curiously, and if I need something to refresh me before going on my way. I'm not exactly sure of the protocol. Do I eat and then pay? Pay first? Plus, I'm a woman disguised in college robes. I am beginning to rethink the intelligence of this idea. But I'm far enough on my way now, and I have to continue on. I ask what sort of stew or pies she has, and she responds that she has a shepherd's pie that just came out of the oven, and also has some beef stew made with a cow that was slaughtered two weeks ago, so it's really fresh.

Upon overhearing that there is a fresh shepherd's pie, several young men who are in a group across the room yell over that they want more as well, so I decide that it must be good and ask for a plate. Plus a mug of mead. The waitress (can I call her that? I doubt it) tells me to sit down and she'll bring it out in a second. She also pours my mead from a jug sitting on a counter behind her.

I sit at a small table by the open shutter (I'd call it a window, but there's no glass, so it's more just a hole cut into the wall, wrapped in a frame), and try to take in my surroundings while I eat. There are rushes on the floor to help keep it clean, and were at one point scented with lavender, but the scent has long worn off. The plate is more of a thick wooden board, and I am given a thick pewter knife, but that's it in terms of silverware. Both the plate and knife look pretty dirty, and I assume they don't have a high powered dishwasher in the back room somewhere.

The shepherd's pie is delicious, though, and I eat it slowly enjoying every bite, and taking breaks for the mead, which is sweeter than what either Matthew or Alice have given me. I am staring out the window and not paying attention to much other than the bustling on the street, thinking how quiet it seems. But then again, it is Sunday. I wonder whether taverns are always open on Sunday's here, or if it's just unique to this one.

I overhear the words "Edward from the college" and perk up, listening while trying not to be obvious. And the heads at the table across from the bar are suddenly all pushed together, and it looks as if they're conspiring about something, or someone. I wonder whether they are supporters of Edward, or not. If only there was a way that I could just go over and ask them. But they wouldn't tell me. And anyway, I'm a woman.

I'm pondering all of this when the pieces of the puzzle fall together. I remember hearing once that there was a tavern near King's where Protestants would gather to discuss the changes they wanted to see. This must be that tavern. The White Horse Tavern. I make a mental note to google it when I'm somewhere safe to take out my phone. If this is the meeting place of Protestant reformers, and they're talking about Edward, they must be worried about him for him to come up in conversation. And even worse, I shouldn't be here. If I'm seen, I could cause trouble for everyone.

I finish up my meal, and take the plate and knife back to the counter, and go back outside, determined to get to my friends as soon as possible. Outside I see a group from the college in their robes, walking towards the market square. One of them is Edward. I keep the hood of the robe wrapped tightly around my face so that I can just barely see out of it, and I walk quickly back to the relative safety of Matthew's rooms and enter without even knocking.

Which is a mistake because the scene in front of me is of Alice and Matthew kissing passionately. I'm about to start fumbling around with apologies when we hear footsteps racing down the hallway. Turning in fear, it is only Harold, but he is sweating and panting from the effort of running to find us. He's received a message from home. Susan is in real labor. The baby is coming.

Alice gathers up her cloak and wraps it around her, rushing out the door with Harold. I follow but before I run after them I take a glance back at Matthew.

"Can you help me with the choir?"

"I think so. I will send you a message."

That will have to do for now, so I nod, turn and sprint to catch up with the two running furiously towards Trinity in front of me. Which isn't particularly easy in these robes. How did people sprint anywhere before running pants, I wonder?

We get to the boat and Alice is jittery. I've never seen her so upset. She is cursing herself for taking the risk of coming into Cambridge when Susan was so close. Harold is calm, reminding her that she thought it was still several days away.

Childbirth is incredibly dangerous for women in the 16th century, and pretty much right up until the 20th. There was a saying that men died in battle, and women died on the childbed. The fact that Susan has been through this four times before doesn't make it any less dangerous. In fact, it could be worse for her because she is older. Alice has her eyes closed and her lips are moving. I know she is praying, and I squeeze her hand and close my own eyes, thinking about the fulfilled and calmly happy woman I just met this morning. Harold is concentrating on punting the boat back as fast as he possibly can, and looks ahead stoically.

CHAPTER TWENTY-ONE

Childbirth

When we get to the village Alice and Harold both jump out of the small boat without securing it, so it's left to me to tie it up, and then follow after them. What I see when I enter the small cottage is terrifying and makes me vow right then and there to never get married and bear children myself. Susan is on her knees on the pallet, leaning over a bench, with her other children still there watching her, looking petrified. No one is available to help her yet, and the oldest, Henry, keeps asking if she needs anything. She looks like she wants to rip his head off, but then she is gripped by another contraction and is doubled over, unable to breathe and screaming for help. The smallest children are terrified.

I see the role for myself in this as I quickly usher the children outside to keep them occupied away from watching their mother go through this agony. I am all for celebrating the beauty and magic of childbirth, but they don't need to see their mom looking like death. Alice rushes to her and starts ordering Harold around, asking him to go back to her house and get rose oil and vinegar for a poultice, boiling water, and finally moving over to Susan and kneeling down beside her, rubbing her back as a contraction hit her. After it passed, she asked how close the contractions were, how long she'd been feeling them, and if she felt ready to push yet.

Then she laid some furs out over the bench to make it a more comfortable place for Susan to rest in between contractions.

I watched all this through the door as I gathered the small children around me, and then we walked over to the open space by the church where I told them stories of a land far far away where machines fly and pictures come alive on screens.

Time seems to stand still, and before we realize it, it's dark. I'm not sure what to do about feeding them, so I bring them back to Alice's home and decide to scrape together whatever we have there for some kind of meal.

While I'm hunting through the cupboards finding beetroots, onions, and a bit of cheese, the children are exploring. I'm not thinking very much about it, concerned as I am with preparing the dinner and thinking about their mother on death's door just a few houses away. But then the second youngest one, Anna, toddles up holding my lip gloss uncertainly. Oh for pete's sake. Nobody in this century seems to grasp the idea of privacy.

Of course they don't. Why would they? These people are brought up in small villages where reputation is everything, and people don't keep secrets unless they're hiding something. Plus there really aren't that many consumer products that one would keep private, unless you were wealthy and living at court, so why on earth would they think about privacy? I get it, but I don't like it.

"Margaret, what's this?" Anna asks, looking up at me curiously.

"Sweetheart," I begin, "where did you get this?"

"In a cupboard. What is it?"

I walk over to where my bag of things is on the verge of being turned over and rifled through. The kids have found my secret stash of stuff, and now I've got some explaining to do. I don't even start to think about the implications if they tell their parents about all this stuff. I think again that next Saturday really needs to work out because staying here another week is going to be pretty tough.

"Children, don't go through those things. They belong to a very wealthy cousin of mine in Ireland, who gave them to me when he was visiting me in Glastonbury, and asked me to keep them safe because he had been given them by Irish elves."

There, that sounds plausible.

They all look up at me with wondrous eyes, trying to figure out whether I'm lying to them, or telling the truth. Of course it's the truth, I assure them. And we mustn't go through other people's private possessions, or the elves might come back for us, I elaborate. I'm really starting to spin a tale here. Now I can hear them, telling the other children when they're together playing, about this amazing stash of magical things given to me by elves. As if I wasn't already weird enough here.

I quickly put everything back, and the children scatter around the rest of the house. "Now go outside and play while I prepare some supper." They protest that it's too cold, and they don't want to go play because they want to see the baby coming. I assure them that as soon as their mother is able to show them the baby, we will find out. In the meantime, they need to eat, and play, so that they are strong enough to help their family in the next few weeks.

The dinner, such as it is, goes on the small wooden table, and the children sit around with me, talking. They are imagining what the baby looks like. They are imagining how cute the baby will be, and how it will coo. I go over to the hearth to add more wood to the fire I started when we first got back, and which is now finally starting to take off. They are still talking away, over their bread and cheese and vegetables. I notice how well behaved they are. The boys aren't throwing things, for example. Every once in a while they try to get me to tell them more about the Irish elves, but

I insist that it's a secret information, and I don't even know that much about it. Then I sit on the stool nearest to the fire and pull out my knitting.

So this is what it would be like to be a mother here, I think. The children at the table eating, me sitting on the stool doing needlework or knitting with wool I carded myself. What a strange life. I notice the children yawning, and think how late it's getting. The children can sleep in Alice's bed tonight, I think. As they are finishing up their supper, I start to herd them over to bed and tuck them in, telling them more stories about the secret lands far far away where there speeding vehicles called trains, and screens where you can talk to your friends even when they are in a different country. The children drift off, one at a time, and my mind starts to drift away to the ideas about how I will get back home, when there's rustling at the door.

Alice enters the room looking pale and exhausted. It's been about seven hours since we left her and Susan. I look up expectantly at her, waiting to find out how it went, and whether the baby is a boy or girl. She just sits at the table staring into the fire, picking at some cheese.

"Alice? Would you like some water?" I ask. I know she must be exhausted.

"Oh Natasha," she lets out a sob, and calls me by my modern name. "She's gone."

What? Susan?

"The baby wasn't coming. She was stuck. Her head was so big."

The story comes spilling out in between sobs. A baby stuck in the birth canal. A mother who had delivered four other living babies without any problems who, for whatever reason was unable to get this one out. The pushing - the unbearable pushing until the mother - Susan - had such a fever and was unable to try any longer. Finally, Harold saying it was ok to try to save the baby over the mother. "It's what she would want," he said gruffly before going back outside, taking a last look at his wife, his face showing no emotions. Then, the emergency c-section, only it wasn't called a c-section then. Alice simply cut into Susan's belly, holding back the tears, her face nothing but professional, and miraculously was able to pull the baby out as Susan died.

The baby girl who was now sleeping in the folds of Alice's bloody cloak.

I took it all in, her tiny perfect fingers and face. Then I looked at the other children sleeping in Alice's bed. Tomorrow morning they would find out that the birth of their baby sister had caused their mother's death. Death in childbirth was common enough for women here, I knew. It was the closest you could come to death. Since women didn't have any kind of reliable birth control, many women could make it through several deliveries like Susan, but as they got older it was more difficult for their bodies to continue. Even Henry VII's wife, Elizabeth of York had experienced this, I thought. She bore a good brood of living children, and then died in her late 30's when delivering another one. Just like Susan, I thought.

What would Harold do? I assumed the children would be comforted by members of the village who would help raise them, but what about Harold? Would he remarry soon to have help caring for the children? And what of this baby sleeping in Alice's arms?

I reached over and took it out of the cloak so that Alice could rest. She looked healthy. Not like someone whose delivery could have caused such pain. She was still bloody and covered in gunk, not having been washed properly. I walked over to the fire and got some water from the kettle that Alice always kept nearby so that she could have warm water when she needed it. I poured a bit into a wooden bowl, and, staying close to the fire so the baby would stay warm, I sponged her off, uncovering her a piece at a time - an arm here, a foot there, and washing her clean. She woke up once and looked up at me curiously. She didn't fuss. The warm water probably reminded her of being back in her mummy's tummy.

I completely forgot about getting home. For the first time I experienced how all consuming caring for a child can be, and I was spellbound by her tiny fingers as I washed the blood off them with an old cloth. I was mesmerized by her perfect eyelashes. Her wonderful little lips and her amazing toes. Looking at a newborn, even one who had been through a rough delivery like she had, was magical. It was like the big bang - this amazing lifetime of possibility, all contained in this teeny tiny little speck of a human. What would she do with her life, I wondered. Who would she become, with no mother and a family that would probably resent her. Would she overcome that, and become a success, at least as much as a 16th century woman could? Or would she flounder? Maybe not even make it to adulthood?

I watched Alice passed out with her head resting on the table, and the children sleeping in her bed. And then I spread out my furs and took the tiny little bundle of life into the warmth with me and cuddled her.

She woke up hungry a few times, her tiny little cries barely waking me, and I had to improvise with milk, using some goat's milk we had, and feeding it to her off my finger. It wasn't perfect, but I hoped it would be ok.

Alice went back out early to get Harold and talk with the local priest, who would want to know all the details before the service to bury her in consecrated ground. Word hadn't yet spread through the village, but it would soon.

I had just put the baby back into a modified bassinet in my furry bed after feeding her when the other children woke up and wanted news of their mother, as well as breakfast, in that order. I wasn't sure that I was the best person to tell them about their mother, but I was the only one around at the moment.

The baby started crying, and the children realized it was with us. At first they looked around, thinking their mother was hidden somewhere in the small cottage. When they realized she wasn't, the oldest put it together and understood that there had to be a reason why the baby was here rather than with their mother. And that reason could only be that Susan couldn't take care of the baby. She was either very ill, or dead.

"Has mother died in the child bed?" he asked, point blank.

The others, who had been chatting, all stopped and looked up at me. This was really not the way I'd imagined this going. I sat down on a stool and pulled them all to me, ignoring the crying baby for a moment.

"Children, I'm so sorry."

That was all I had to say. The look on my face said the rest. The oldest ran from my attempted embrace, out the door back to their home to check on his mother. The younger ones began to cry. I held them to me as their wails joined those of the baby, and for a few moments I tried my best to comfort them. I was a poor substitute for anyone else in the village, who would have been so much better at this than me. But I did my best, and with the toddlers leaning in to me sobbing, I walked over to my cot and lifted up the baby so they could see.

I had this whole idea that the new life would be somehow comforting in the face of such loss, but I was wrong. They didn't want to see her. They wanted nothing to do with the baby who killed their mother. I cradled it to me, and dipped my finger in the pail of goat's milk to let it suckle on. I was so worried about the germs and the lack of refrigeration, but there was nothing else I could do, and so my finger kept going into the pail of most-likely-rotten milk, and back to the baby's mouth. When she calmed back down, I walked them back to their home.

It was a short and somber walk, and we were seen by several people out milking cows, or feeding chickens, or doing the sorts of morning things that people do here. They saw me holding the baby, and the children crying, and they understood as well what had happened. The men took off their hats, and the women just looked down at the ground, knowing that there but for the grace of God, they could go.

Chapter Twenty-Two

The Party Expands

When we got back to the cottage I called for Alice or Harold, but neither answered. I opened the door, and there on the table I saw Susan, laid out in the same clothes she was wearing yesterday, of course, and looking like she was just having a rest after a long journey. The children ran to their mother, and even though I'd only met her yesterday, I choked back tears as well.

Being a woman in this time period really sucks, I thought. If you don't do all of this - the marriage, the family, the risk of death in childbirth, if you want to do something else, then you're seen as odd, strange, and maybe even a witch. I wanted to go home. I held the baby to me, and looked down at her sleeping face, her perfect little lips open as she slept. I wanted more for her than this.

"Children, where should I put the baby?" I asked, reluctantly. I didn't want to let this little pile of goodness go.

"We don't want her," Henry looked up from his mother's side where he was clutching Susan's hand, and responded instantly.

"What do you mean? She's your sister," I tried to respond gently.

"No, I mean it. We don't want her. We can't take care of her. She killed mother. Father won't want to see her."

The other children all looked at me blankly, and I couldn't tell whether they agreed or not. But either way, I wasn't going to leave her with this brood of children who didn't want their beautiful sister.

It felt very odd to be having this discussion over a dead body. So I acquiesced.

"I'll take her back with me," I said.

"You can just keep her," said Henry.

I didn't want to leave them alone in case something happened, but I also didn't want to intrude on their private time saying goodbye to their mother, so I went outside and leaned against the wall. Eventually I saw John, the waterman who had taken us to Cambridge to market the first time, walking past, down to the river. He would know what to do.

"John, hello," I approached him.

He looked up and gave me a grin. With icy blue eyes and a rugged complexion he was actually very good looking, I thought. If I had to stay here, I could do worse than being with him. I'd have to keep that in mind. What a funny thought.

"John, I have such sad news. Susan has died giving birth to her daughter," I said.

"I assumed as much when the house was so quiet. It's sad. She was a good woman," he responded, and made the sign of the cross.

"Yes, the thing is, I have her baby here."

John looked in at the tiny little human I'd been keeping close to my body to fight off the cold.

"They don't want her. The children don't."

"What a miracle that Alice was able to save her," John said immediately.

"Yes, but what do I do with her?"

"I suppose you keep her," he responded nonchalantly, like it was no big deal. "They won't want her, I'm sure. You can either leave her out and hope someone gets her, or you can keep her. She looks like a sweet little thing," he peeked over the folds and took a look at her.

They were all talking about her like she was a stray cat or something, rather than a small perfect human being. I didn't understand this place.

"I know you're not from around here," John started out. "We're not cruel people. It's just a matter of what's practical. You can't let your emotions come into it."

I nodded. I understood his point. I guessed I would have to talk with Alice and figure out what to do. There must be some kind of procedure for this. She would know what to do. In the meantime, I'd take the little baby back home, and do what I could for her.

Just then I saw Alice and Harold walking down the path with another man, who I'd assumed must be some type of undertaker, and they disappeared into the house. Alice gave me a weak smile as she passed through the doorway, and I heard the crying as Harold greeted his children. Then I took the little newborn home. This must be a much more common scene here than it would be for us now. Life just goes on, even in the face of such sadness.

When I got home, I laid the little babygirl down on my cot, and started to have a look around for something I could use as diapers. I found some old clothes, and did my best to try to wash them, and then I went back over to where she was sleeping, and laid down with her and rested my own eyes.

I woke up an hour later to a messenger sliding a piece of vellum under the door. It was from Matthew, a note saying that the choir could meet me the following afternoon, as well as Thursday. He had planned the 3:30pm service for Saturday. Things were officially on.

With all the sadness working out the logistics of a new baby in the past 24 hours, I had almost forgotten about Matthew, and the fact that I was still trapped here. Now that I had an idea of a way home, I was both excited and nervous. The first thing I needed to do was memorize the music so that I could teach it to the choir tomorrow. We were living in the days before printed copies, and the choir would be expecting to memorize their music. What I was going to give them, though, was much different than anything they had ever sung before. Hopefully, with any luck, they wouldn't even have to sing the entire piece. I would be long gone before the final crescendos. Hopefully with Alice and Matthew at my side.

Then the idea hit me. If I was already getting fake documents for Alice and Matthew, just maybe... I looked down at the little baby laying on the furs beside me. Maybe I would be able to take her, too? I needed to talk to Alice. In the meantime, I would memorize the music, and make sure that I could teach. I got my iphone out, pulled up Spotify, and started the music. At the same time, I got to my email and looked at the pdf of the score Sophie had sent, as the music was playing.

It wasn't the most difficult piece ever, and I was becoming immersed looking at each line, and knowing it really well. The weather had turned colder with rain starting to come down again. The baby woke up once to be fed and changed, and I used one of the rags I'd found, and the goat's milk. The rest of the day passed, and it was dark by the time Alice finally arrived home, exhausted. I was still pouring over the music, but was feeling more confident about it by the minute.

Alice wanted to simply eat and then fall asleep, but she did me the courtesy of talking to me first. I had been in the house with the baby all day, and had no idea how things had gone with the priest. Alice told me they had taken Susan's body out, and it would be buried the next morning, in the church ground. Harold was doing ok; was just trying to handle the logistics of being alone with his four children. She didn't mention anything about the baby. I asked her what would be done with her.

"Harold doesn't want her," she said simply. "I suppose she'll go to a home for foundlings in Cambridge. Sad, I guess. She seems a sweet sort. But they can't afford another one, and who will look after her now?"

"Alice, couldn't we keep her? Couldn't I take her home with me?" I blurt it out without even thinking about it.

She looks at me, a bit stunned.

"You would try to take her back with you? To your time?"

"Yes. She would have so many more opportunities than here. I have some savings, I have money to be able to support her. I can do it," suddenly I realize that I am devoted to this little creature, and I need to figure out a way to be with her and give her the best life possible. I understand how people can fall instantly in love with their babies now. She's not even my baby, but I am washed over completely with love for her.

We both look over to the pallet where she's sleeping. Alice looks serious, and thinks for a while.

"Let me talk to Harold, to make sure he really does want to give the baby up. If so, I will tell him I've given her to someone who can care for her. But what if you don't go back? How will you care for her here? Have you thought about that? Life is hard enough on your own."

I pause for a moment. "Let me think about that after we've seen whether it will work, ok?"

Alice sighs and rests her head on her chest with her eyes closed for a few moments. "I knew her so well. She was one of the people who cared for me after I came here. She was an amazing woman, and the world is worse off without her."

"I'm so sorry, Alice," I begin. "But I can take her daughter and give her opportunities that Susan couldn't have even dreamt of. Even if I do stay here - once I figure things out in the short term, I will be ok. I know what's going to happen, remember? So there's money to be made in knowing the future. Susan's legacy will be her daughter thriving. I can do this, I know I can."

It's as if suddenly I have found my purpose. Those gorgeous blue eyes looking up at me have told me everything I need to know. My reason for being is to love and support this girl, and I'm going to do everything I can to make a success of that.

And my first order of business is to continue memorizing these lines so that I can teach the choir tomorrow. I fill Alice in on the choir practice schedule, and the service on Saturday. "If you come along, we can raise her together," I remind Alice. She just sighs. I know, she can't think about anything right now. Not with the death of her friend so freshly on her mind.

I go back to Spotify and my pdf copy of the score, singing through each line in my own range, listening to the music and comparing the notes. I do this over and over, memorizing each part completely, because I know that I won't have access to the music or the recording tomorrow. I can't imagine how the choir would react if, midway through the rehearsal, I pulled out my phone and queued up the music. They would all faint, I think.

The evening and overnight goes about as well as a night with a newborn can be expected. She woke up several times to feed, and each time I dipped my finger in the goat's milk and let her suck on it until she seemed satisfied and went back to sleep. Sitting there in the dark with her falling back asleep on my chest, I thought about what I needed to do when I got home with her. I was going to have to figure out getting her to a pediatrician soon. I was sure there were vaccines she needed. I would have to get papers for her.

Make her legit. Make up a story. I could say I adopted her, which was true.

I dozed, falling back asleep with the baby on my chest.

Chapter Twenty-Three

Rehearsals

Tuesday was another rainy grey morning, and I greeted it with a mixture of excitement and sleep deprivation. There was no coffee available, and I was sorely missing it, especially now that I was caring for a newborn. We still hadn't named the baby girl yet, as Alice was trying to confirm that Harold really didn't want her, but given his lack of interest in her so far, it seemed a good bet that he didn't.

Everyone was preoccupied with Susan's funeral, which had been that morning, and no one seemed to be giving a second thought to this new little bundle of wonder. I was growing more attached to her by the moment. Her beautiful blue eyes looking up at me, her tuft of fine dark hair, and her perfect little mouth making sweet cooing noises were all enough to make me fall head over heels in love with her, and each day the love grew exponentially. I could barely think about what would happen to us if we didn't get back. I couldn't let my mind go there. I needed to use all of my depleted energy to focus solely on the rehearsals that were coming up today, and the journey home. Next week at this time we would either be home, or we'd still be here. If we were still here, I'd deal with it then. For now, every thought was going towards getting us home.

I felt very secure in the music, and now I just needed to figure out how to teach it to a Renaissance English choir. I wasn't a choral director. I had sung in choirs, but not since college. I wasn't sure how people even conducted choirs right now. I would show up early and talk with Matthew, and hopefully he would be able to catch on to the music as well as me, and I would count on him to do most of the heavy labor.

I spent the morning holding the little baby girl, who mostly slept on my chest, and making plans. I texted Sophie to let her know rehearsals were starting, and that Saturday was definitely on. I also updated her on what was happening with Susan, and threw out the idea of bringing the baby home. To which she simply responded that I was insane, but we'd figure it out once we got home. Then at 2pm I bundled up the baby in blankets, and wrapped her in my dress so she could be warm against my skin, and waited for Joseph to take me back to King's. I think about how modern women pack giant diaper bags for short outings with extra outfits, and tons of extra diapers and wipes, baby lotion, formula, everything under the sun. I just have a small sack with a tin of goat's milk, and some extra strips of cloth which were doubling both as diaper and swaddling outfits. I'm a minimal kind of mother, I guess. Forced to be, but I'll admit that it makes life simple.

The baby slept the entire way to King's, and only woke up as I stepped off the boat. She cried for food, and I rushed down to Matthew's rooms, hoping I could feed her there in peace. He was still recovering, but he looked much better than he did two days ago. I filled him in on all the events in our little village while the baby drank the goat's milk off my finger. Susan's death and the little girl who is now so tied up in my heart, and my story. Matthew listened to everything, and after I was finished with the story he said a prayer for both Susan and the baby girl, laying his hands on her as she looked up and cooed, which I thought was incredibly sweet. I told him I wanted to take her home with me, and he just shook his head.

"You'd take us all back with you, it seems."

"Just those of you I love and who I think would do better in my time," I responded. He smiled.

"So, about this music..."

I reached in my bag and got my phone, and queued it to the music, while also bringing up the pdf of the score for him to study. He looked at the way the music was printed in amazement - its lack of beauty was compensated for the uniformity and clarity of the notes. Together we listened, and I taught him the parts he found challenging. His reaction to the music was what interested me the most, though. He was still blown away by the miracle of recorded music coming out of my little phone (though to be honest, I still am, too - I haven't grown up with iPhones). And he adored having the score so easily accessible. But he questioned whether all of this accessibility took some of the miracle and the mystery out of everything.

Music is so mystical for him. Having it so easily available might take some of the wonder out of it. Like having Christmas every day of the year. I supposed that it was true, even in my lifetime I've come to appreciate books and magazines much less than when I was a kid, and a trip to the bookstore was a huge deal. Now I have the opposite problem: 1000 books on my kindle I'll probably never read, and more music than I can ever listen to. Maybe he was right. But I didn't really want to think about the alternative; having music be so special and so unavailable. There had to be a happy middle, I thought.

At 4pm we all went into the Chapel, both Matthew and I feeling confident in the music, and me especially gratified that he was as confident as he seemed. The choir entered, most likely curious about what was happening that they were being called for a special rehearsal. The choir was comprised of 16 voices, including men and boys singing the high soprano and alto parts. Matthew introduced me as a visiting musician, but took control of the rehearsal from the start.

It wouldn't have been proper to have had a woman teaching the music to men, and so Matthew explained that I was from Glastonbury en route to Ely and that this was a new piece that I had learned there, which I was taking to the Cathedral in Ely. It was a brand new style of music, never heard before in England. So new, in fact, that we didn't have music. The choir would have to learn it by heart. There was some grumbling at this, but not as much as you would expect. Choirs were used to memorizing music in the Renaissance.

Matthew sung each part for the first two introductory O Magnum Mysterium's and then put it together for the full choir. The sound was rough, but the notes sounded right to my unprofessional ear, and I still got goosebumps thinking about the fact that this legendary choir was singing a contemporary piece. Someday I would have to get hold of Morten Lauridsen and try to tell him my story. If he'd believe it, I think.

I sat in the choir stalls as Matthew progressed, one phrase at a time, calling on me when he wasn't sure of a note. I snuggled into the baby, and listened to the music, feeling as magically transported as I had that first day, only I was still here. Hopefully on Saturday everything would align again and the magic of this music would take me back home.

The rehearsal lasted about 90 minutes, and by the time it was over, the choir seemed to be pretty confident of the music. I was certain that after Thursday's practice time as well they would perform it to the same high standard that the choir performed it 500 years later when I heard it.

After rehearsal Matthew and I went back to his rooms while he fetched Joseph to have him take me home. I could tell that the rehearsal had exhausted him, and he didn't want to talk and go over everything in minute detail, analyzing each singer's face and attitude towards me. I knew back home Alice wouldn't be in much of a mood to talk either, even if she was at home, which wasn't likely given how much she was helping Harold with the children. I nuzzled into babygirl. "I know it's totally inappropriate, but I'm going to wind up confiding in you, I guess. Sorry." She just kept sleeping, happy to listen to my stories as long as she was being fed.

Back home, as I suspected, Alice was still at Harold's. I knew this morning had been the funeral, and I hadn't attended. I walked over thinking I would pay my respects and see how everyone was doing. When I knocked on the door, Alice answered. Seeing me with the baby, she simply said, "you should go." I heard Harold asking who it was, and Alice responded that it was just a peddler. At that point Harold came through and saw me standing there, with the baby, and exploded.

"You would dare to bring that evil piece of Satan into our house after she killed her mother? I should never have allowed her life to be saved. Take her away, please," he begged. Then he turned and went back into the house.

I stood there gobsmacked. He called this little perfect bundle of wholeness and love a piece of Satan? Alice simply smiled gently. "He really doesn't want her," was all she said.

I walked back to Alice's house feeling so alone and empty, and knowing that now, more than ever, we needed for Saturday to work.

I wash the dirty diapers in the warm water by the fire, fix some food for myself, and pass out with the baby, gently promising her that I will make everything right for her. She's not a piece of Satan. She's a blessing. She's my blessing. She's a piece of joy given to me, a precious piece of life that I am going to cherish.

I stay in the house the rest of the week, except for the one rehearsal on Thursday. We're nesting, the baby . I imagine that this is what it must be like for mothers in all times. The first few weeks just spent sleeping, feeding, washing diapers, and getting to know the baby. Word gets out that I'm going to keep her, and a few people bring blankets and other things, but most see her as an added burden, and they don't know me anyway, so there's not really much reason for them to offer much neighborliness. She and I spend hours looking at each other, gazing into each others' eyes, sussing each other out.

By the time we venture out on Thursday for rehearsal, I'm feeling a lot more confident, both as a new (though completely unexpected) mother, and for our plan. It feels like rain is coming, which is just what I want. The choir sounds amazing. Even Matthew is looking much healthier. Conditions couldn't be more perfect for everything to work Saturday, though when I ask him what he's thinking about with coming back with us, he is noncommittal. As is Alice.

CHAPTER TWENTY-FOUR

Saturday

I am overjoyed on Saturday when I wake up and it's raining. Very similar weather to how it was just a handful of Saturday's ago when I woke up the day after Halloween with a splitting headache. That night was spent here, for the first time, in Alice's, in 1539. I take a moment to reflect on what has happened over the past four weeks. I've gone to church services regularly. I haven't had alcohol, unless you count the mead (I don't). I've studied and learned about physics, Einstein, and I've stretched my brain in ways it hasn't been stretched since I had just moved to England and was taking everything in with bright eyes and the enthusiasm of one who hasn't become jaded to life yet. I really like this new me, and I want to keep developing her. I want to continue on what I've built here. This life of reflection. I want to spend Friday nights reading and going to concerts of the music I love rather than going out and getting drunk and wasting my life away. I want to spend weekends at museums. I want to spend the mornings meditating rather than grabbing the nurofen and coffee to try to get me to a state where I can face the day. I like who I am here. I just want to be who I am here, but in my time. Maybe I could even start to move past the pain, find some forgiveness for myself, and possibly even learn to let love in again. Don't go getting too ambitious, I laugh to myself.

I luxuriate with Paddy next to me purring, snuggling into the furs. I've always been antifur, and they are a bit scratchy, but these things are incredibly warm. I think that I am going to spend more mornings enjoying snuggling with cats under my duvet when I get home, and then I stop myself. I'm assuming that it's going to work out, and I don't know for sure that it will. I need to not get my hopes up too high so that if it doesn't work I'm not totally destroyed. This seems like my best bet, and it seems like it "should" work, but lots of times even when things "should" work, they don't, and I need to accept it if this turns out to be all for naught. Plus, I won't be able to spend a lot of time grieving, because I'm going to have to figure out my next move. Like, how to survive when my protector seems to be in deep shit.

Alice starts to stir, and I realize that she's been quietly thinking as well. She still won't tell me whether she's going to try to come back with me, but I see her grab the burlap sack we made and put it by the door, so I'm assuming she'll try to take the animals in that, just in case. We quietly eat our breakfast - the bread, cheese, onion and beet, and then go out to feed the chickens and check on the livestock. She talks quietly to each animal, and I think that she must be telling them that she may not be back, and that either way they will be well cared for, and she loves them.

I can imagine her telling them this, and so I give her some space. I make sure I have everything I need as well, and I snap some pictures of Alice's place on my iphone, just to show people back home what it's been like. Well, to show Sophie anyway. And maybe Julian the physicist. I'm not sure who else knows, and I don't want that many people to know anyway, so I'm going to keep it mostly for myself, for sentimental value.

On the way down to the dock, with the baby wrapped in my dress, we go over the plan for the day again, as if we haven't rehearsed it a hundred times already. The music, the timing, where we'll be sitting. Alice forces the struggling cats into the sack, clearly against their will, and then we depart. She keeps looking back at her house, and I'm becoming more certain that she will try to come along with me. "It's going to be safe there," I tell her. She just nods at me and looks a little frightened. There is a boat there with Joseph, just as Matthew said there would be. We get in, but we don't talk. We watch the world go past, and I think that hopefully the next time I see this view, it will be without water because they will have drained the fens, and it will be 2015.

We arrive at King's around noon. I text Sophie to ask her if she is en route to Cambridge. She texts back that she is, and she's brought clothing for all of us. I love her a little more every day. We sit in Matthew's rooms going over the service again, and finally at 3pm he says it's time to go out and greet the choir.

We have told people about this special service, and there is already a queue to get in. I see Edward, and some of the other monks, looking very put out by this, and they mention it to Matthew.

"Have we even received permission from the Bishop for this," they wonder and mutter. Matthew always responds that we don't need permission from the Bishop to do what our remit is, which is to bring the word of the Lord to people, and to bring them comfort and news of great joy the way the angels did to the shepherds during the time of Christ's birth.

I pick the spot where I'm going to sit, and I try to match it up so the view is exactly what I had seen before. It's a big deal, and it would really suck if I was in the wrong place, and the person next to me wound up going back to 2015. But I've practiced this before, and I know where I'm meant to be. Today isn't about thinking. We've been thinking and practicing all week. Today is about instinct and trusting my gut, and my gut places me in this spot, so in this spot I shall stay. The baby is peacefully sleeping. Alice sits next to me. And we wait. We wait while the public filters in. I am grasping my bag, and Alice is holding tight to her precious cargo on her lap, who are squirming, but not as much as I'd thought they would be.

"Did you give them something?" I asked.

"Just a bit of nightshade in their morning meals," she responds, and strokes the sack lovingly.

And finally, the moment comes. I look outside and it's still raining, just as it was all those weeks ago. The light looks similar, though it's darker. It would be, it's a month later in the year. I hope that doesn't affect anything. I hear the choir beginning the opening hymn and starting to process down the Chapel. I wait during the opening prayer, which sounds suspiciously like a Protestant one from the Book of Common Prayer. I wonder if Matthew has taken a peek at my phone without me knowing it and has looked up the liturgy that will be on its way under the next monarch? I wait throughout the Bible readings. The rain is still pattering. The public seem to really enjoy the Evensong service, and I feel happy that they got to have this experience, though frankly I don't really care about them right now. As Matthew walks down the aisle to lead the choir in singing the O Magnum Mysterium, the one which I pray with every bone in my body will take me home, he walks past me and drops a piece of vellum on the floor without even a glance in my direction or Alice's. After he goes, I reach my foot out to take it. Just then, in the silence of the Chapel, I hear noise. I hear boots, and I hear shouts as men try to enter the Chapel.

Edward, standing in the back, runs to let them in, and shouts, "Heresy! Traitors to the church! Matthew is supporting and having carnal relations with two witches!"

There are some gasps and shouts, but Matthew looks nonplussed and, though he seems to turn white, he keeps the choir singing. He has told the choir, I'm sure, to keep singing no matter what, and I pray that they reach the chords I need before Edward arrives with his gang of thugs. I'm not even sure which chord it is that I need, and the piece is six minutes long. It definitely won't take six minutes for these men to reach us, and I realize that this whole thing has been so stupid. I really don't want to be burned as a witch or a heretic, and I don't want Alice to suffer. Or Matthew. What have I made them do for me? I feel so guilty. I should have just gone off to London to try to make it as a book binder or something. I can read; that would be a skill here. Why did I drag them into this?

I see the face of Richard Chancellor, and it all makes sense now. He has told the men who are trying to bring Cromwell down about me, and about the plan, and he wants to try to make a good impression on the new leaders by bringing them a heretic and breaking up a heretical ring in Cambridge, a main seat of learning. What an asshole. He seems to have forgotten that the next monarch, who will fund his voyage of discovery, is a strong Protestant. I see him pointing to us, and I see men with pikes and, oh crap, swords coming our way, glistening off the candlelight in the darkness.

But then.

Then the world gets peaceful. Completely peaceful. There is only the music, and the feeling of Alice clutching me. Alice is clutching me! Just that thought makes my heart slow down a bit. Whatever we go through, we won't be alone. The world starts to turn dark, but it could just be the sun setting early, as it does in winter. I still see the men coming my way, but it doesn't matter to me. They can come, but I know now that they won't reach me. No matter what happens, they aren't going to get to me.

The music is continuing, and the chords are vibrating inside of me. I feel nauseous again, and I recognize the feeling from before. It wasn't nausea. It was the music, the vibrations, causing me to lose consciousness and moving me through the prism that separates each time from the rest. And then, just as I black out, I feel another hand. I saw Matthew walking towards me too, but he seemed to also be moving in slow motion. I'm not sure who it is; I can't see them. I can only feel the hand on mine. Well, whoever it is will get a shock they may not have expected soon. But I don't care. I really don't care about anything right now. I just want to sleep. And I allow my head to fall down on my chest, on top of the baby's head (oh, the baby's head!) and then my entire body slumps forward. I feel Alice holding tight on to my arm, and then it's just black.

CHAPTER TWENTY-FIVE

Results

Next thing I know, I wake up on the floor with a circle of tourists around me. They're wearing retro-looking clothing, and I'm worried I've wound up in yet a third time, like the 50's or something. That would really suck, especially if I brought Alice and Matthew with me. Hang on, did I bring them. I look both ways and I don't see them, though I still feel the baby wrapped in my dress. I'm really starting to worry, especially as people are starting to look at me and talk amongst themselves. I see poodle skirts. I swear to God I see a poodle skirt. I'm feeling very confused, and I catch a glimpse of the Reubens painting at the altar, and then suddenly the world goes black again.

Well that was very strange, is about all I can manage in my head before things start swirling around again, and then there are the hands on me, and I hear voices. I hear Sophie. God bless Sophie. My eyes are still closed but I can hear her saying, "move along, move along, nothing to see here. Just a re-enactor who got a little drunk and got lost. Nothing we haven't all seen before."

And then I feel Sophie's hands under my arms, cradling the baby as she helps sit me up. Oh my God, I'm home! I don't even want to get up, I just want to sit here with my eyes closed and bask in the wonderfulness that is being home. Being in my own time. Surrounded by the people who know me, by a culture I can understand. Oh my word, it feels heavenly.

"God, you smell," I hear Sophie say.

"What was it like, Oh I must hear all about it," a man starts talking quickly - way too quickly for my current state of mind, I think. That was rough. I don't remember it being as rough the first time, going back.

"I haven't had a bath in a month," I muster.

Then, "where are your friends?"

"Are they not here?"

I open my eyes. I don't see them. Oh my God, what happened to Matthew and Alice?

Shit, what have I done? Are they back there getting pummeled by soldiers of Stephen Gardiner and the conservative Catholics? Is Alice being tortured? What about the animals? Oh please God, please let them be ok. I'm a little bit numb, thinking about it. How can I ever find out what happened to them?

I'm still laying on my back, and we are starting to attract some attention. I see someone in a red robe headed our way, which can't be good. Sophie helps me up and starts to pull me out of the Chapel. We go through the organ, and out the door to the right, towards the alleyway, not the courtyard, and they both help me, as I'm still faint and stumbling, and we wind up on the grass outside the Trinity library, by the side of the river.

I sit down, and start to gather myself.

"Are you the physicist?" I ask the man.

"Yes, I'm Dr. Julian Breen," he responds. "Such an honor to meet you, Natasha. You have no idea how much I've been looking forward to this. You must tell me all about it. We can write a book, perhaps."

I look at Sophie, pleading.

"How about if we let her catch her breath just a bit before we start asking her a load of questions."

"But what happened to Alice and Matthew? How can I find out?" I look at Julian for the answers. He seems to know a lot about wrinkles in time and whatnot.

"I'm afraid I don't know. Can you tell me about your journey? How did it happen?"

I reach for my phone to look at the time. It's odd to me that only ten minutes ago I was worried for my life because Edward and the pikemen appeared. I can't find my phone.

"My phone is gone," is all I can muster. My phone, with the memories, with the pictures of the hut, with the proof of my visit. With the pictures of Matthew and Alice, my friends. I'm heartbroken. I wonder if it got lost during the journey.

"I think I stopped off somewhere," I say. "Like the 70's or something. It was really weird. How could that have happened?"

"Well, you were traveling through the dimensions so very quickly," Julian responds. "you were passing through time at light speed, and it's possible that you were stopped along the way."

I lay back in the grass, thinking that just this morning I came in on the river to the dock at King's, wondering whether I'd ever see home again. And here I am basking in the cold December afternoon outside the Wren library, which didn't exist when I was here before. I saw this college being built, though. What an honor, I think. There must be a way to be able to check on Alice and Matthew, though. It's all well and good that I'm safe, but there has to be a way to make sure they are. An idea comes to me.

"Sophie, call my phone."

"What?"

"Call it. I want to know where Alice and Matthew are."

Sophie pulls out her own phone, and calls me. I hear it ringing, and then I hear, "where are you dear? We'll be over as soon as we can."

"Alice?"

"Eleanor, dear."

"Eleanor?"

"Are you near the Chapel? Thomas and I have been waiting in the market to see when you would arrive. We have some of your things in your room, still. You can come back and change and have a bath and cup of tea."

Thomas? Eleanor?

Hang on. It sounds so familiar. My bag? My room?

Oh my God. The old people who had the bed and breakfast where I was going to stay. By Parker's Piece. With the giant tub. Oh my God, that was Alice! I thought there was something familiar about Alice. But I still don't understand.

"Dear, we'll tell you everything when you tell us where you're at! Are you by the river?"

"Yes, the backs, outside the Wren library."

"We'll see you in a few moments."

I look at Sophie and Julian.

"the story is about to get a little more interesting," is all I can say. Meanwhile Sophie starts to lay out the clothes she wants me to change into, and is wiping me down with deodorant wipes. "Sophie, I can't just change here, for the love of God. I have a room at their place with all my clothes and stuff."

"I'm just thinking about getting you back over there. You really do stink." She holds up a mirror to me. Funny, I haven't really looked at myself in a month. Alice certainly wouldn't have had a mirror. I didn't even think about it. But now, seeing my face, I notice that, in addition to the dirt that is literally smeared in various places on my skin, I also have cheekbones that I didn't have before.

"Have I lost weight?" I ask, to no one in particular.

"A month on root vegetables and dry bread... yes, you have lost weight," Sophie responds.

I continue to examine my face from all angles. My eyes look brighter than I remember them.

There are no dark lines and bags underneath them, like I've always had before. A life of hard work in the country seems to suit me. Perhaps I shall move to the countryside and buy a pig farm or something like that. But a place with a lovely shower, I think. That would be the best of both worlds.

Just as I am analyzing my gray hairs, I see the couple walking around the corner, holding hands and looking so happy. I get up and run to them, and we all fall into each others' arms in a big hug, crying and laughing, and squishing the baby who has woken up and is also crying, at the same time. They look exactly as they did, only forty years older.

"How did this happen? Are you ok? How did you make it? What happened?" questions start tumbling out of my mouth, and they hug me to them and laugh.

"Come back to our house, and we will tell you everything! My, you look so ragged. I forget how dirty we were, Thomas."

Thomas chuckles. "Well, you were. I was a scholar, remember?"

"Let me see the baby," Alice insists. "Have you named her yet? I forget whether you had by this point?"

I hadn't, but I have now. She is baby Alice.

They throw a coat over me, and walk on either side of me, hustling me back to their house, which I remember was very close. Sophie and Julian walk behind, and it's like I'm in a trance. I'm so confused. But they appear to have been safe, which is all that matters. And I'm home, which is also all that matters. And I have a baby, which is another thing that matters. Other than those three things, nothing else matters.

I'm completely overwhelmed walking through the market square. There are so many people. So little shit in the streets. So few animals. So much noise. So many bikes. There are so many voices and horns and cell phones and I never realized how loud it all is. I literally can't even hear myself think. And then we pass the Marks and Spencer food hall. Oh Lord, I want it. All of it. I suddenly feel hunger like I've never felt before. The hunger of someone who has experienced gluttony, then been without and thought they'd never be able to binge again, and then sees the opportunity to go crazy one more time. I want to devour the Marks and Spencer food hall.

CHAPTER TWENTY-SIX

Eleanor, Thomas, and Alice

"Sophie, go in there and get me food, please" I half-order-half-command. Suddenly I want every sort of cake and piece of chocolate I can find. Honestly, it's like I've been on some kind of sugar fast. Which, I guess I have.

"What do you want me to get?"

"Chocolate rolls. Lots of chocolate rolls. And other cake sorts of things. And bread. And Diet coke. Get me all the diet soda you can find. And coffee. Oh my god, I want coffee. And berries. And ice cream. Lots of berries. And oranges. Just get me three of everything. And underwear. I need new underwear," I call after her.

She looks perplexed, and then gives a snort as she walks into the store, getting Eleanor's address so she can catch up with us when she's done.

We continue to walk, me holding on to the baby, my baby, my baby Alice, who is looking up at me, taking in everything, being so good and still, even after what we've all been through. I'm aware of feeling the stones on my feet, which still have the leather wraps around them. People are staring at us, but I really don't care. They can look. Maybe they think I'm homeless. Hell, maybe I am. I'm not sure how much I have left in the bank, but I'm guessing I don't have a job anymore.

We get to Eleanor and Thomas' house and I immediately expect to be sat down and told the answers to everything. But Eleanor insists that I go bathe first while she watches the baby. I don't need to be asked twice, and so I kiss Alice's nose and then skip up the steps. Eleanor gives me every sort of soap she has, and tells me to take my time, and she'll be up with a cup of tea in a minute. I take off my scratchy wool dress and shift for the last time. I sit on the edge of the tub and unwrap the leather on my feet, and then turn the water on.

I look at myself in the mirror. I'm hairy. Kind of neanderthal-like. I've definitely lost weight, and I have more muscle. I'm absolutely filthy. There is dirt underneath my fingernails that I don't think is ever going to come out. And in all the little wrinkles in my skin. It's from sleeping on those furs, I think. They were warm, but covered in filth. My hair is stringy and limp. It's desperate for a deep conditioning treatment.

But I really do look healthier than I've ever looked before. At least since I was a teenager. I look strong. I look fit. I examine myself from all angles, and with one last look decide to say goodbye to the dirt for good. I sink into the warm water, which is a few inches deep at this point. I've added bubblebath, and close my eyes, basking in the heavenly scent of magnolias and the warmth of the water. This is amazing. This is seriously the best thing in the world.

Eleanor comes in carrying a tray of hot chocolate and McVitie's and my stomach jumps at the sight of the spread. The hot chocolate tastes like heaven, and the chocolate biscuits crumbling in my throat are golden beams of light that are making my insides all shiny and happy. I sigh with happiness.

"I'm going to let you go now, dear," Eleanor says. "And when you're ready, come down and we'll tell you everything."

"But Alice, why can't you just tell me now."

"Oh, Thomas will want to tell some of the story. And please call me Eleanor now, love. Alice was a lifetime ago, and now Alice is your daughter," she adds. My daughter. My baby Alice downstairs.

With that, she leaves closing the door behind her, and I'm looking up at the angled ceiling through the skylight at the rain. Always the rain here. I feel grateful for the roof, and for the warm water, but I'm feeling a smidgen sentimental for the thatch.

The rain picks up and the sky gets darker. I hear voices downstairs as Sophie comes back and coos over the baby. It's 4:40pm. Two hours ago I was still incredibly nervous and afraid that I might be stuck in 1539 forever. It's so much to take in.

Eventually the water starts to get cold, and I notice a filmy layer of grime now that the bubbles have all gone away, and I suspect it's time for me to get out. I'm anxious to hear the story now that I'm reasonably clean, and am missing baby Alice, so I shower off and ask Sophie to bring up my clothing. Oh, the feeling of soft, warm, comfortable, contemporary clothing. I may never get out of yoga pants again. And my warm cashmere cardigan. A piece of paradise that I get to wear on my body. Lucky me.

Once I've cleaned up my mess, and thrown my old clothes into the trash bag Sophie so kindly provided (she vetoed my idea of donating them to a museum for the authentic cloth), I head back downstairs, where Julian and Thomas are getting to know each other quite well discussing black holes, while Eleanor is holding Alice as she sleeps. There are three bags from the Marks and Spencer food hall, and I'm about to devour it like I haven't eaten in a month. Which is kind of true.

I sit down on the couch and everyone looks at me.

"Why are you looking at me?" I ask. "I want to know about them," and I point.

"Well, it's just that you look so different when you're not filthy," Sophie jokes. "So much prettier than you did when you left." I smile at her and have to admit that I had already noticed it and I agree.

"I want to buy a pig farm," I declare.

That gives everyone a chuckle, though I'm not sure why.

Finally Thomas and Eleanor finally tell their story.

"We wound up in 1978 when you opened your eyes for that moment. We both let go of you because we thought we were in the right place. But then we realized we weren't."

"But go back a minute. Matthew, I mean Thomas, why did you decide to come along finally?"

"I had dropped the note to you, which was actually a note saying that I wasn't going to come. It's probably still in your bag. It told Eleanor - Alice then - that I loved her, and I wanted to spend my life with her, but I just couldn't leave academia, studying the Word of God, trying to reform the church, and that I felt my life's work was there. You'll read it. But then, when Edward brought in the men, and I realized that we had been betrayed by Chancellor, who must have really known which way the wind was blowing, I was afraid. It wasn't just that, though. I realized that I could never do the things I wanted to do in Cambridge in 1539. I wasn't going to be able to reform the church. Not in my lifetime. Not after what you'd told me. I really wanted to see this time in the future you had talked about where people were more liberal and more accepting, and where women had equality, and men walked on the moon, and all of the other things. I mean, knowing that exists, how could I pass up an opportunity to see it? And so I told the choir to keep singing, to not stop under any circumstances, no matter what happened, and I took a chance that it would work."

"And you?" I look at Alice. "What made you decide? I figured you were sticking with me by how tightly you held on, but what made you finally choose to come?"

"Same as Thomas, I suppose. I knew there wasn't going to be much for me to live for if Edward was going to be running the university. I depended on Thomas way more than I could have ever imagined. And you had put this idea into my head that I could do something more fulfilling, study and get a degree, and make it on my own independently, and it was exciting. I wanted to see if it could work. I knew what I had there, and I wanted to try something different."

"So," Thomas continues. "We let go when you opened your eyes, and then suddenly we separated from you. We had been holding on to each other, though, so we were still together. We arrived in 1978, and we were scared to death! People gathered around us to make sure we were ok, and we could hardly understand them, the language is so different. I will admit, we cursed you for several weeks after we first arrived." They look at each other and laugh.

"We managed to make it to the market square, and we realized that we were in your modern times, but we looked at a newspaper and saw the date, and realized that something had gone horribly wrong. We didn't know how we would ever be able to re-stage something so grand again to try to make it work to get to you, and anyway, who knows where we could have ended up then. So we begged for food and money for several days." Eleanor takes a breath, remembering the hard times, I suppose.

Thomas picks up where she left off. "We slept rough until we found a church charity. They gave us new clothing, and some meals, and we had decided that we would make up a story saying we were from a foreign country, because we knew we could never pull off being actual English people here. We would have to have some kind of excuse for why we talked differently and had such strange accents. We didn't know of many places to name, but we had heard you talk so much about Russia, so we said we had come from Russia. Of course the idea now that we would have made it out of the Iron Curtain into England without being noticed in any way is absurd, but the people at the church believed us and helped us. It was obvious we weren't a threat to anyone, and we clearly didn't know which way was up, so they took pity on us. I started studying philosophy and religion thanks to a scholarship for immigrants, and Eleanor studied to be a midwife," he looks at her proudly. "We changed our names because it seemed to make sense. We were in a new place, with a new life, and it seemed strange to keep our old names."

"Anyway," Eleanor continued, "we realized the first night that we had your phone, which must have come out of your bag, but we had no idea how to work it. We just kept it with us until technology caught up to it."

"But how did it get to me, then?"

"We swapped it for your actual phone the day you were here, before you left for Evensong. We knew it would be the same as the phone you were using. It must have been since it was your phone to start with."

"So there were two phones?" My head is starting to hurt again. Even Julian The Physicist looks perplexed at this, and I see him scribbling some notes in his notebook.

"Anyway, enough about the phone," Sophie interrupts. "How did you guys ever survive?"

Thomas tells us more while Eleanor soothes baby Alice, who has started to fuss a bit. "Well, it wasn't that hard to learn modern English. Since we were meant to be Russian, nobody expected very much of us, and we were given a lot of grace to make mistakes and mess up. We studied the newspapers so we knew what was happening in the Soviet countries, so we came up with a convincing story and were given passports and birth certificates. We eventually became British citizens, and then we married in 1984. I graduated from Corpus Christi college with a PhD in comparative religious studies, and Eleanor got a job in a maternity ward, and spent her life delivering babies until she retired when she was 60."

"And did you have children?" I ask, wondering and hoping and keeping my fingers crossed at the answer.

"Yes, we have three." Eleanor says, beaming and pointing to the pictures behind me on the end table. "Two girls and a boy. All doing well. All studying at, or graduated from Cambridge colleges."

I'm so glad for them. It warms my heart inside to know that their story became so happy here.

"We always wondered how we would meet up with you. Of course we knew that it had to happen, otherwise our story wouldn't have happened in the first place, and we knew the date. But when you called us from the station wanting the room, it thrilled us because we were going to see you again after so many years! That was why I was asking you so many questions. Of course I had heard your story during our month together, but I wanted to hear it again, from you, and see you in your modern element for the last few moments before you went back to our time."

"So you were happy here," I asked. "It worked out? You're glad you came?"

"Of course we're glad!" they both answered in unison.

"We never could have had a life like this at home," Eleanor says. "Not that I don't miss it. If I would have had a family there, or anything that would have kept me there besides just myself, it would have been really hard to leave. But as it was, it was just me, and I was happy to try an adventure. I have had a profession here. I've spent 25 years delivering thousands of babies, and getting to know the mothers, and doing what I love. I never could have done this back home. And Thomas has written papers on church history and books on the Reformation." she says proudly. "Also, we never could have married then."

But my biggest burning question still hasn't been answered.

"What about the animals?" I wonder. "what about my love Paddy and the others?"

"They made it just fine. They kept us warm the first few weeks sleeping rough," she laughs. "They survived for several more years and then started to pass, one at a time."

Baby Alice starts crying then, and I panic for a minute. What do I do here? I don't have any formula, and all I know how to do is dip my finger in fresh goat's milk. It all suddenly seems so complicated, this world I'm entering of diapers and wipes and teethers. But Eleanor saves the day again, handing me the baby and fetching a bottle and formula. "When you arrived, I bought a can of formula because of course I knew that you were going to try to bring her." She nods over at Alice. "We didn't know, of course, whether or not she would actually make it. We prayed she would. We knew she wasn't with us in the 70's, and we knew we had made it, so we felt confident that she would arrive with you, and we would need to provide you with the items you'd normally get at a baby shower." She smiles, handing me the bottle, which Alice hungrily sucks.

"She's still feeding well," Alice notices. "I can help you find a doctor and have a check up."

I look over at Sophie. "Yes, we're going to need a birth certificate for her. And how am I going to explain to everyone that I suddenly have a baby?"

"You've been away for a month. There are those reality shows where the girls don't even know they're pregnant," Sophie says happily. "We'll get a birth certificate figured out, and for a few weeks people will wonder, but then they'll just be blown away by her gorgeousness," she adds, cooing at Alice who is still eating happily, her eyes closed in a feeding stupor.

I start to panic. "But you guys, what am I going to do?" Suddenly the responsibility of what I've signed myself up for seems so much more daunting than it did this morning, and five hundred years ago. "For money? Long term? What will I do?"

Ever practical, Sophie has an answer. "You'll rent out your house and you'll move in to a smaller flat. You can get a scholarship and go back to school. It'll be all right. We'll all help you."

Alice drifts back to sleep on my chest, and I cradle her little head. It will be ok. I know it will. I'm encircled in this little orb of love, surrounded by these people who will help me, and I in turn will keep my arms wrapped around little Alice, and the two of us together will take care of each other. That is one thing of which I am completely confident. I smile at them all, and feeling exhausted myself, I allow my head to drop.

As I doze off, I hear comforting voices in the background. Sophie telling Eleanor all the various baby gear she thinks I'm going to need, and what she can give me of hers. "She'll need a wrap for sure. So much more convenient to have your arms free.

And a good stroller. She can have mine. It's just collecting dust now."

There's also Thomas's soft voice talking to Julian about how it felt to let go of me, and land in the 70's. The sensation of dizziness.

It's good to be home, I think, before falling completely asleep.

CHAPTER TWENTY-SEVEN

Epilogue

I dropped little Alice off at her school this morning. It's a chilly September morning, and she's wearing her dear sweet cardigan with the patch of the school crest. This was her first day away at Big Girl School, and saying goodbye to her broke my heart a little bit. I watched her until she was all the way inside her classroom, waving to me and blowing kisses out the window.

"I'm so excited for school!" she exclaimed this morning. "It'll be an adventure!"

She has no idea the adventure she had before she was even a week old.

I turn from the school and walk back to our flat, the second floor of a row house in Cambridge, on the far side of Jesus Green. We're happy here, in our little village. I'm finishing up my Master's in Musicology at Sidney Sussex College, thanks to a government grant for new mum's, and my thesis is about the changes in liturgical music of the 16th century. If I'm lucky, I'll be able to get a job teaching with my degree, which, now that Alice is in school, will be good for us both.

Alice hasn't really asked about her father yet, and I'm not sure what I'll tell her when she does. We left it blank on the birth certificate. The hospital barely batted an eye when I showed up with a six day old baby, and Eleanor at my side saying that I had gone into emergency labor and delivered at home. They asked me a few questions, took my blood pressure, made sure we were both healthy, and Eleanor signed the birth certificate as the delivering midwife. Which, of course, she was.

Eleanor and Thomas have no grandchildren of their own yet, so they dote on Alice as if she was theirs, and she eats up all the affection. We spend every Sunday with them, going to Evensong service at King's after the big Sunday lunch. Sometimes Sophie comes up with the children, and Alice loves playing with her "cousins." We've cobbled together this little family of love, and for right now, it's enough.

We never travel in time again.

I never had my meeting with Howard.

HISTORICAL NOTES

The Protestant Reformation in England turned out to be one of those historical pieces of magic where everything lines up just perfectly. Henry VIII was named the Defender of the Faith in 1521 by the Pope Leo X because of a treatise he wrote blasting Martin Luther. If Katherine of Aragon, his first wife, had carried a surviving male son and heir, chances are that Henry would never have entertained the idea of leaving her to marry Anne Boleyn. The concept of breaking away from Rome, and flirting with the new Protestant ideas would likely have never entered his mind.

But, Katherine didn't carry a living son, and Henry did upend religion in England so he could marry Anne. He was also tempted by the money of the Church, and so through Cromwell and his other ministers, he dissolved hundreds of monasteries and convents throughout England, reclaiming the land for the Crown and using the money to build a navy, and make war with France. Anne also didn't have a living son, but did give birth to the future Elizabeth I, one of the greatest English monarchs who would usher in a "golden age" of arts, Shakespeare, exploration of the Americas, and military defeat of the Spanish Armada.

But Elizabeth only came to the throne after her two siblings before her died. When Henry VIII died, still worshipping in the Catholic tradition, his son Edward (by Henry's third wife, Jane Seymour) inherited. Edward was raised strongly Protestant, and was surrounded by Protestant advisors, so England swung rapidly towards a period of intense Protestantism. But Edward died after only six years. Next to inherit was his older sister, Mary I, the daughter of Katherine of Aragon, who was staunchly Catholic. She tried to reunite England with the Pope, and bring back the old ways, including the Latin Mass, and Catholic practices like praying with a rosary. Then she died.

Suddenly Elizabeth was the Queen, and while she famously didn't want to "make windows into men's souls," she did demand obedience, and so Catholics who refused to attend her Protestant services, known as recusants, were persecuted and fined, and many Jesuit priests were killed due to suspicion that they were foreign agents.

The thing about this time that fascinates me is how it would have affected ordinary people. There are people who would have been born and brought up with one spiritual tradition, who found their monasteries and convents (places that provided medical care, schooling, and hospitality) gone. Then the world shifted strongly to Protestantism. Then back to Catholicism with the previous form of worship considered heretical. Then back to Protestantism. By 1558 when Elizabeth inherited the throne, someone who was in their mid-40's had come of age in one tradition, seen it outlawed, then had it return, and then outlawed again. I can only imagine how frightening and frustrating that must have been, if you could even keep up with it.

In 1539 Henry VIII was getting ready to marry his fourth wife, Anne of Cleves, and cement an alliance with the Protestant German princes against the Catholic forces of France and Spain. That marriage didn't work out, and his chief advisor, Thomas Cromwell, who had organized the marriage and was a leading reformer, found himself on the receiving end of the King's wrath.

His enemies had seen to it that he received the blame for the bad marriage, and Cromwell soon lost his head. The conservatives were trying to make a comeback.

Universities then, like now, were often seats of new liberal thinking, and the White Horse tavern was a meeting place for Protestants throughout the city.

I have taken huge liberties with the daily life in a university Chapel, and for that, I apologize. Given that the book involves time travel, which is also highly unlikely, I hope the reader will forgive my indulgences for the sake of the plot.

To learn more about this time period, I would self-promotionally direct readers to my podcast page for the Renaissance English History Podcast, at http://www.englandcast.com where you can get book lists, listening lists, and movie recommendations, as well as podcast archives on subjects close to this book (including music and the religious turmoil). You can also subscribe to the new episodes, which tend to be biweekly.

ABOUT THE AUTHOR

Heather Teysko is a writer whose Renaissance English History Podcast is one of the top indie history podcasts on iTunes today. She also puts out a regular Tudor Minute segment on YouTube. She moved to England when she was 24 because she was in love with English choral music, and wanted to immerse herself in the history and music. She spent every weekend making pilgrimages to Evensong services around the country. For ten years she worked for California's largest library consortium, most recently as the Assistant Director for Innovation and Development where she led a project to build an open source library eBook platform.

Now Heather lives in Andalusia, in southern Spain, with her husband and daughter, Hannah Zen. This is her first novel, though she has also published a memoir of her infertility journey and the loss of her son, Fragile and Perfectly Cracked, under the name Sophie Wyndham.

You can learn more about her and contact her via her podcast website at http://www.englandcast.com

or facebook.com/englandcast;

or follow her on twitter @teysko.

Printed in Great Britain
by Amazon